Ann Summers

Madame B's Lost in Lust

Ann Summers

Madame B's Lost in Lust

EBURY
PRESS

1 3 5 7 9 10 8 6 4 2

Published in 2007 by Ebury Press, an imprint of Ebury Publishing

A Random House Group Company

Text written by Siobhan Kelly © Ebury Press 2007

The Random House Group Limited Reg. No. 954009

Addresses for companies within the Random House Group can be found at
www.randomhouse.co.uk

A CIP catalogue record for this book is available from the British Library

The Random House Group Limited makes every effort to ensure that
the papers used in our books are made from trees that have been legally
sourced from well-managed and credibly certified forests. Our paper
procurement policy can be found on www.randomhouse.co.uk

To buy books by your favourite authors and register for offers visit
www.rbooks.co.uk

Typeset by Palimpsest Book Production Ltd,
Grangemouth, Stirlingshire

Printed and bound in Great Britain by
CPI Cox & Wyman, Reading, RG1 8EX

ISBN: 9780091916480

CONTENTS

FOREWORD

I'm thrilled and delighted to welcome you to *Lost in Lust*, a red-hot volume of explicit, enthralling true stories told to us by real women. We've hand-picked these tales from hundreds of real erotic confessions told to Madame B. I'm so proud that they celebrate women who do the things you want to do - but would never dare.

There's a world of erotic adventuring for you to enjoy within these pages. I hope you have as much pleasure reading these stories as Madame B did compiling them. I'll let her tell you more.

Jacqueline Gold

Ann Summers, CEO

Welcome to a fourth collection of tales to titillate and tease, awaken and arouse you. The following pages contain true stories of women who turned their sexual fantasises an orgasmic reality.

Every woman has at least one sexual confession to make, and whenever I make a new friend I'll eventually ask what hers is – even the shyest open up in the end. My genuine fascination means I'm an avid listener, and I relish every explicit detail. When the story has been told, I steal away and write it all down in my little red-leather notebook – a journal so crammed with steamy, sizzling stories that it's almost hot to the touch.

Now I've decided to publish my favourite true confessions. Keep this book by your bed by all means – but if you read it last thing at night, be warned that sleep will be the last thing on you mind!

Happy reading,

Madame B x

MIDAS

Long-distance love takes imagination to make it work. Phone sex and email flirtation isn't the same as having a warm body to reach for in the night. Sometimes, it's even better.

When Mark comes home with a bunch of flowers and a sheepish look on his face I know that he's got to travel for work again. This is the third time in as many months that he's left me on my own for a week while he goes off to client meetings all over the world.

'So where is it this time?' I ask him sulkily, offering him my cheek, not my lips, when he bends down for his kiss. 'Tokyo? Seattle? Munich?' I turn away. I don't mean to be snappy, and really I should be grateful: Mark is six foot two of gorgeous husband: funny, sexy, faithful, and a right horny little bastard. He would be perfect if only he were here a little more often. His job in IT sales means we have our gorgeous home, and also means that my own salary is pretty much pocket money. Because of Mark I have an amazing lifestyle. So I really shouldn't complain.

I just miss him so desperately when he goes away. I can't sleep alone, and my God, the sex! I miss the sex. Five years into our relationship, I thought it would have tailed off by now, but it's become deeper and more intense than it ever was. And to go without him for ten days, another ten days, well, it's just unthinkable.

'Baby,' says Mark, drawing me into his arms and combs through my hair with his fingers, a tender touch that melts me inside. Even when I'm trying to sulk and be angry with him, he knows just which buttons to press to calm and soothe me. 'It's only for a week this time. We can talk every day. I'll miss you too, but it won't be for long.'

'When are you going?' I say, looking up into those handsome green eyes of his.

'Tomorrow,' he says, looking guilty again. 'But I'll make it up to you.'

He kisses me again, and this time I don't resist, let his tongue slip between my lips and probe my mouth. When his hand goes between my legs I'm more than ready for him. We peel off each other's clothes with more urgency than usual, aware that this is the last time for seven days. We lie on the bed for a couple of minutes, just kissing, that's all he has to do, and before he's even touched my clitoris I'm spreading my legs as wide as they can go, showing him my soaking slit and telling him how much

4

I want him. And then he's in me, filling me up like no one else can.

Let me tell you about Mark's dick. I don't know quite how, but it's as if it was made for my body. The first time I felt him inside me, it was like I was complete for the first time in my life. It's a pale biscuit colour, it stands upright above two smooth, even balls. It's long, but what I like best about it is its girth: every time he presses against my pussy with that smooth, rounded head I know he's going to be inside me, stretching me pleasantly, moving around and probing every inch of my cunt.

And that's what I'm feeling right now as my pussy muscles hug and massage his hard-on. Mark pulls out a little bit and drives into me with a force that borders on aggression because he knows that I love, live for, those moments when he first gets inside me. He does this for maybe two, three minutes, watching my face, reading the signs of my body. He knows just the right moment to trip me over the edge into my climax with his finger on my clitoris. As I reach my orgasm, it's bittersweet and my contractions force him to come, too. We hold each other for a while, drift off to sleep with sticky sheets and limbs, smelling of each other's bodies.

When I wake up it's 4 a.m. and Mark is packing his case ready for his early-morning flight. He leans in and kisses me goodbye. I show him that my nipples are hard and reach for his cock but he shakes his head, there's no time. Last night's fuck should have me satisfied for the lonely days ahead, but on the contrary, it's just left me more frustrated. Mark's dick is addictive: the more I have it, the more I want it, need it. I hear the door close behind him and manage to grab another couple of hours' sleep.

When I wake up again, it's 8.30 and I'm dangerously late for work. I throw back the bedclothes, jump in the shower, dress and hop in my car, just about making it to my desk in time for my 9 a.m. meeting. But I might as well have stayed at home. All day I think about Mark, replaying what happened last night, wondering how I'll get through the next week till we can do it again.

When I get home to the empty flat, I take off my work clothes and slip on one of Mark's T-shirts. It still smells of him. At the foot of the bed, I notice what looks like a black shoebox tied with a gold chiffon ribbon. I must have been in too much of a hurry to see it this morning. Mark often buys me gifts on his travels, but he's never left one behind before. Intrigued, I pluck the little gold card that's tucked into the bow. His elegant handwriting, a stark reminder of his physical presence, makes me ache for him.

'I've had this for a while now, darling,' it reads. 'I've just been waiting for the right time to give it to you. It should stop you getting too lonely while I'm away.'

In the box, wrapped up in gold tissue paper, is a

sleek gold mobile phone. It's switched on but no one has called yet. But there's more to my gift than a new phone. Wrapped in even more layers of crinkly paper, I giggle and squeal with delight to find a life-size, gold-plated model of Mark's erect penis. I run my hands over it, marvelling at the lifelike details. It's definitely him, I'd know it anywhere; that's the vein that runs in a little squiggle from the tip to his balls down the right side, even that tiny triangle of skin under the head of the penis where he loves me to put my tongue is there. I press the tip to my lips, touch my teeth to it: it's cold and metallic and it makes me feel hot and horny. Automatically, I lift the hem of Mark's T-shirt and use the tip to prod my clitoris and shiver with delight as it becomes engorged and sensitive.

That's when the phone rings. It's a long number starting with the code for a country I don't recognise. I pick it up and Mark's voice is there, crackly and intermittent, but it's him, calling me from the other side of the world.

'So you've found my present?' he says, his voice loaded with meaning.

'I love it!' I squeal excitedly. 'But how did you . . . ?'

'I had to stick it in a plaster mould in an artist's studio,' he laughs. 'Then they made a gold model of it.'

I think of Mark slapping his dick into a tray of wet

plaster just so that I might have a cast of him, and the mental image is touching and arousing.

'I thought of you while I was wanking myself,' he continues. 'And I thought of your pussy and I got really big and hard, and then I stuck it in the plaster. The guys at the studio did the rest. Afterwards, I went straight to the toilet because the thought of you with my golden dick in your pussy made me so hard I had to wank immediately.'

I'm picturing the scene and I realise that I've been gently stroking and tapping the tip of the dildo on my clit rhythmically. It's hard and demands stimulation. My flesh is hot and wet, and the cold metal feels delicious.

'So where are you now?' says Mark.

'On our bed,' I say, sinking back into the pillows, phone in one hand, dildo tightly clasped in the other. The soles of my feet are pressed together, my legs making a diamond shape so that my trembling pussy is exposed. Looking down, I can see the tip of my clitoris protruding from between my cunt-lips. Gently, so gently, I press the tip of the dildo – Mark's dick – on my clit and rock it from side to side. I can't help it, I let out a little moan of pleasure.

'Tell me what you're doing,' he orders me. 'Put the phone on speaker.' I flip a switch that casts his voice out so that it fills the whole room. The mobile is on my pillow, and Mark's there with me. He breathes like he's just been running, and

I picture him in his hotel room, his hand working the shaft of his gorgeous penis in long, firm, hard strokes.

I fight the temptation to shove the dildo inside me right now, and instead I listen to Mark's voice on the phone, giving the orders.

'Lick the tip of it,' he says. 'Now draw it down your body, circling your tits.'

I obey him, pressing the dildo to my lips and moistening it with saliva before dragging the smooth, slippery surface down on to my warm breasts. I tell Mark that this feels good – really fucking good. He makes me draw circles around my nipples and I watch, fascinated, as they swell and darken the way they usually do under his hands. The gold dick is hard and shiny against the soft velvet of my skin, and makes little dents in my tits which spring back when I pull it away. We carry on like this for about five minutes until I'm so turned on I can hardly stand it. I notice my thighs begin to shake, a sure sign that all the tension in my body is building up and that it's going to spill over soon.

'Please baby,' I whimper, close to begging him. 'I need you inside me.'

'Well then,' he replies, and in the background I can hear the slap of his hand on his dick. I love the thought of him jerking and tugging his dick while its likeness penetrates my slit. 'Talk me through it,' he says.

'Okay, I'm on the bed, my legs are apart and my pussy . . . is on *fire*,' I tell him, encouraged by his breathing which grows more rapid by the second. 'I've got your hard, solid dick and it's just outside me. I'm putting it in. The tip's in. It feels amazing, but I'm holding back. I'm just twisting it a little. It's cold inside me and my pussy's so, so wet. I'm sliding it in and out of me, in and out. I can't get it deep enough, it feels so like you, it's big, and it's hard, and I'm fucking myself, my pussy's just throbbing.'

I start using my free hand to play with my clit, fingers working fast and furious over the slippery little bean.

'I can't hold on much longer baby,' I say, or rather I scream because I'm right on the edge now. My free hand travels all over my body, I tear at the flesh of my thighs, maul my own tits in frustration, keep frantically rubbing my clit and I tell Mark all of this in explicit detail until his voice interrupts me.

'I'm coming,' he shouts. 'I'm coming hard, I'm coming so fucking hard,' and then he lets out this long, low moan. It's the noise he always makes at the point of orgasm but it's so much louder and more intense than I've heard for a long time. The sound of it flips a switch inside me and I come hard, working my clit with a finger either side of it and with Mark's big gold dick inside me. I slide my knees together, wincing as my thighs close and envelop my still-tender flesh. Using my deepest muscles, I push the dildo out. It lies on the bed linen, its smooth gold surface marbled with my pussy juices.

'That was amazing,' I whisper breathily to Mark. His own voice sounds equally sleepy when he replies, and I know that he too is spent and feeling tender now that the crucial moment has passed.

'I knew you'd get off on it,' he says. 'I'm rather proud of myself for fucking my wife from another country.'

'So will you call me same time tomorrow?' I ask.

'I can't wait. Of course I will,' he says. 'Oh, and baby? That phone you're holding – it can take videos. Learn how to work it. We'll do the same thing again – but this time we'll be able to see each other.'

We say goodbye and hang up. Immediately I experiment with the phone, looking for the video function. Isn't it *marvellous* what they can do with technology these days?

HIRE LOVE

Hannah is rich, powerful and in control. Everything in her life is organised to perfection. Hiring a male escort for the night, she assumed that it would be a simple business transaction. She hadn't prepared for the way he made her feel when he held her close. When a woman like Hannah finally loses control and surrenders to her desires, the results are explosive . . .

There's a lot of pressure in my line of work to look right, to live a certain lifestyle, to have the whole package. Much of my six-figure salary goes into maintaining this image. I've a wardrobe full of designer clothes, a city-centre loft apartment with off-street parking for my Porsche and membership to an exclusive gym where personal trainers keep this power-dressed body buff. And usually I've got a man, a handsome, rich man to go with it all. What's the point of working all hours, preserving this hot, powerful self-image if there's no decent Alpha-male-fuck in it? Well, that's the ironic thing . . .

Last year, I'd been working so hard that my love life had taken a back seat for a while and there'd been no decent man in my life, or bed, more precisely, for at least six months. It was one of those periods where you're so busy, you haven't even the time to ask yourself, hey, when did I last go on a date? How long is it since I last had sex? Even my rabbit vibrator felt neglected in those days. At night, I'd be working on my laptop in bed, if not flat-out after a drinks party where networking, not pulling, was the main focus. My bank balance and achievements were so healthy that I wasn't too worried about being single. Career was my number one priority for now, there would be plenty of time for fun and games later . . .

But my firm's Christmas ball is a big deal. You simply *have* to take a date. And I'd always had the best dates of any woman in the firm. I'd walk into the ballroom with an amazing man: a model, an actor, a personal trainer, a millionaire entrepreneur, a F1 racing-car driver. But that year, I had no one to take with me. And I didn't want to turn up alone.

A week before the big day, I realised I would have to act fast. With so much time taken up preparing for the ball itself – shopping for a fabulous dress, extra hours in the gym, manicure, blow-dry, make-up artist etc – I certainly wasn't going to have time to meet a new guy. So I resorted to my little black book of fuck-buddies. As I scanned the list of names and international numbers, I felt a frisson of excitement, remembering the good times – and great sex – I'd had with many of them. I'm still on good terms with my flings and exes, so surely one of them would want to join me at a fabulous party in one of London's smartest hotels?

The first person I called was Jermaine, a male model I took on holiday and fucked for a week in St Tropez a few years back.

'Hannah!' he had picked up the phone clearly delighted to hear from me and keen on the idea of partying, but when I gave him the date of the ball: 'Oh, damn, baby, I'd love to so much but I have plans that night.'

It was the same story with Ewan, the racing driver. He was obliged to attend his sponsor's annual party that evening. Hey, from a corporate point of view, I totally understood, so we hung up having made plans to meet (ie, fuck) in the New Year. While the thought of getting re-acquainted with Ewan's gorgeous dick in January was enough to warm me in the Christmas chill, I still didn't have a suitor for the party. One by one, all the boys in my little black book had prior engagements – well, it was mid-December. I cursed myself for leaving things until the last minute. Normally I'm so together.

I called Jane, my colleague and best friend, to see if she could hook me up with anyone. I've never known her to be without a date – and they're the only men even better-looking than the ones I bring along. I hoped I could rely on her to do the sisterly thing. 'What? At this time of year?' she scoffed. 'You've got to be joking. Everyone's diaries are totally full.'

'I know. It's fucked-up. What am I going to do?' I asked her.

'Same thing I always do,' said Jane. 'Call Adonis.'

'Who?' I said, not sure I'd heard her right.

And then my best friend, about whom I thought I knew everything, confessed that for years she'd been using a high-class male escort service. As she described the agency, it became clear that it was the best-kept secret among the richest women in London. The escorts on its books, mainly models and actors, were intelligent, highly attractive, well-bred young men charging hundreds of pounds an hour for the pleasure of their company. And, as Jane pointed out, unlike a real date, they were doing it professionally and so delivered to a standard. No risk that they'd get drunk and embarrass you, be a crashing bore, or get aggressive on the doorstep about 'coming in for coffee'.

I tried to recall the last few men I'd seen with my friend: they had, without exception, been charming, witty and devastatingly handsome. No way would I ever have guessed that they were paid escorts. I was impressed. And Jane – beautiful, rich and glamorous – was hardly the desperate type. I wrote down the telephone number and website that she dictated to me. After I hung up the phone, I fixed myself a martini and gave the matter some serious thought. I was used to spending my money on the best of everything in life. I've paid out top fees for ski instructors, Harley Street doctors, top colourists for my hair . . . even my cleaner costs me a bomb but came highly recommended. So why should the service of good-quality male company be any different?

Out of curiosity, I looked on the website and signed in using the password that Jane had given me. The navy and gold design was sleek and professional, and I could choose my escort by any category I wanted: location, race, age, IQ, height, even educational background. I didn't know where to start, so I decided to browse the guys based in London. There were about fifty of them to choose from; each had provided a head-and-shoulders photograph as well as a full-length picture in a suit and – my personal favourite – a shot in his underwear. Each boasted an impressive CV. I'd been expecting a parade of male bimbos but there were a wide variety of guys from former professional footballers to part-time diving instructors, and there were even a couple of university professors.

It was like a grown-up girl's version of the best toy shop in the world. I scrolled through page after page checking out images of sexy guys: no wonder the agency called itself Adonis. I looked at the rates: okay, £500 an hour *was* pretty steep, but I was blowing a grand on my dress and with the bonus I'd just received, I could afford it.

I narrowed my choices down to a final three. There was Marlon, a gorgeous black model with cheekbones that you could cut glass on; his shot was from an ad campaign I'd seen in magazines. I turned him down, though: if I recognised him from his modelling work, maybe others would too. Paul was next, a dirty-blond surfer type who was a fireman four days a week. Physically, he was more my type than anyone else on the site but, as higher education was missing from his CV, I'm afraid the snob in me turned him down. The company ball is an event demanding a gentleman walker who can talk confidently about books, art and culture. And then there was Olivier, a French-born, London-living PhD student who, his blurb said, worked as an escort so he could enjoy a good standard of living and still follow his academic pursuit of archaeology. His underwear shot showed that he had beauty as well as brains: his body was lean but muscular and his black hair brushed his collarbone. As I looked at his picture I could just imagine what that hair would look like falling into his eyes. Yes, Olivier, I thought, zooming in to get a close-up view of his impressive-looking manhood, you're the one.

I dialled the number on the screen and was put right

through to an operator. I told her who had recommended me. 'Ah, Jane, one of our best customers!' she said brightly. 'Do say hello to her from me, and let her know we've got some great new guys she might want to meet.' I heard her fingers click on the keyboard as she checked Olivier's availability for the next Friday night. 'You're in luck,' she said. 'He's free for a booking. Would you like to proceed?'

My fingers were shaking as I retrieved my platinum Amex card from my Prada purse and read out the numbers to her. I was doing this, I was really doing this. The following transaction produced a rush of adrenaline far outstripping any previous shopping high, let me tell you. I get excited buying a new designer bag, but this was in a different league entirely – I was hiring a *man*. And a very good-looking man, too.

The operator gave me a mobile number to call next Friday afternoon, and let me know the score: Olivier would pick me up in a cab at the appointed time, accompany me to my function, and I'd be charged by the hour depending on how long I wanted him for. I assured her we'd be done and dusted by midnight, 1 a.m. at the latest, and she gave a little laugh.

'That's what they all say,' she said. 'You'd be surprised; a lot of women want the guys stay on even longer.'

Friday rolled around really quickly and I took the afternoon off for some serious pampering. Although I wasn't hiring Olivier for sex, I had a Hollywood bikini wax and wore new matching underwear – a wine-red bra and knicker set – so that I felt sensual and romantic, feminine and confident. I had my hair teased into soft waves that framed my face and caressed my shoulders, and my face done by a professional make-up artist. I had to admit when I checked myself out in the mirror, I looked good: glossy and groomed and toned and rich and successful, every inch the corporate career girl. The final touch was to slither into my dress, a clingy, green silk number with a plunging neckline and a fishtail skirt that made me feel like a mermaid and walk with a sexy wiggle. Just as I was hooking a pair of diamond chandeliers in my ears, the doorbell rang: it was Olivier, right on time.

I buzzed him. 'Come on up,' I said into the intercom. 'I'll be one minute.'

I heard him tell the cab driver to keep the meter running and then the lift door slam shut. I stepped into my heels and was struggling with the clasp on my diamond choker when Olivier rang the bell. Here we go, I thought, taking a deep breath and unlocking the door.

The 3-D reality of Olivier took my breath away. If he'd looked good on a computer screen, in the flesh he was the sexiest man I'd ever seen. The photo hadn't captured that X-factor that makes a handsome man sexy. The computer couldn't quite convey the smooth curve of his upper lip or his strong nose, or the smile he flashed showing white, even teeth and a glimpse of pink tongue. I stood there open-mouthed for a second, more guppy fish than mermaid, my eyes travelling all over his lean body. I found time to notice that his suit was YSL and I registered my silent approval.

'Pleased to meet you, Hannah,' he said, extending a hand. 'I'm Olivier.'

I went to shake his hand and dropped my bracelet which clattered to the floor. I was as giddy as a schoolgirl on her first date. Olivier's smooth, sophisticated sex appeal had unnerved me.

'Allow me,' he said, dropping to the floor to retrieve my necklace. As he bent down, I noticed that his thighs were long, lean and supple. I pictured his sinews rippling under the black of his suit. When he came up to fasten my diamond choker, his fingers on my flesh made me tingle and I felt his warm breath caressing the skin behind my ear. Being this close to a good-looking man I realised just how long it had been since anyone had touched me. My sexual feelings, dormant beneath the surface, began to stir. Oh no, I thought. Not tonight. Tonight I need to be cool, professional, dazzling: I don't want to be distracted by sex!

Olivier held the door for me as I collected my faux-fur cape and clutch bag and we made our way down to the taxi. He was easy to talk to, with a dry sense of humour that I liked immediately.

'So if anyone asks – which they will – where did we meet?' he asked me.

'I hadn't thought about that,' I replied.

'Well, I usually find that saying we met at a friend of a friend's dinner party tends to work,' he twinkled. 'Hearing about other people's dinner parties is so boring, you don't generally get any more nosy questions after that.'

I had been worried that I'd hear the minutes ticking by and fret about what this was costing me, but Olivier was excellent value for money, in fact I didn't notice the hours passing at all. At the dinner table, he was excellent company, more than a match for the high-powered bankers I'd asked him to mix with, giving little about himself away but asking questions that made people feel important, flirting slightly with the other women but always keeping a hand on my arm to show he was with me. At the beginning of the evening, I found this hand a warm reassurance; by the time dinner was over, Olivier's touch was beginning to arouse me.

Two female colleagues approached me in the bathroom while I was reapplying my make-up.

'He's gorgeous,' breathed one. 'If you ever get bored, I'll have him!'

I didn't tell her that he was only a click away. But he'd

had the desired effect: the men were impressed and the women were jealous. I could have left then and I would still have made my point. But I didn't want to. I wanted him to stick around a little while longer.

Liveried servants cleared banqueting tables and pushed them against the wall, turning the long hall into a dance floor. A band struck up a slow, sexy tune.

'Now,' said Olivier, taking me by the hand. 'Now we make them really jealous.'

And he held me tight and swayed me in perfect time to the music. He took the lead, and I let my body follow his rhythm. I felt my shoulders and neck relax for the first time in months as his strong lean arms encircled my waist and pressed my body against his. I felt my expensive panties begin to get damp, aroused by this closeness. As the warmth of his chest against my breasts made my nipples go hard, I wondered if he'd noticed my sexual response system crunching into gear: he responded by placing a hand on my arse, making my pussy pulse urgently. With my head on his chest, I couldn't see his expression, but his hand trailed gently over my arms, shoulders and back with a touch as tender as any real lover. He began to fondle my favourite erogenous zone, the back of my neck, the one spot that's always been guaranteed to get me horny. I don't know why but the skin around my hairline and behind my ears is like a short-cut to my clitoris. As Olivier's smooth fingers played with my earrings and caressed me there, I couldn't help but let out a low moan of pleasure.

Olivier heard that all right and drew away from me. Before he spoke, he glanced down at my eager, swelling nipples and I blushed. 'Hannah, I must say,' he began.

Embarrassed, I tried to cover up my desire, although my glittering eyes and parted lips must have betrayed it. 'Oh, that was *nothing*,' I said. 'I was just, um, sighing, I was . . .'

Olivier interrupted me by pressing a finger to my lips, a teasing gesture that foreshadowed his kiss. I wanted to take that finger between my lips and gently bite and suck it. I tried to calm myself down with some deep breaths.

'What I wanted to tell you,' he said, and as he whispered in my ear, his lips caressed that area of my body behind my neck that makes me go weak at the knees, 'is that if you want to take this further, that's fine. It's usual for me to offer "extras" to a client. We charge the agency for the time we spend until now, and then you pay me in cash for any personal time we spend together. And with you, Hannah, I'd be only too happy. Would you like me to take you home?'

My mind was saying, Hannah, there's a line between hiring an escort to a function and paying a man for sex. It makes him a prostitute, and it makes you . . . what does it make you?

Another little voice in my head said, oh, but how *thrilling* would that be, having a man please you! And it's so straightforward, no bullshit, just there to do your sexual bidding.

But both of these voices were drowned out by a rush of blood to my head, my pussy, my tits, so that my body made the choice for me. I nodded meekly and with that he took his finger away from my mouth, ran it slowly over my lower lip and then pressed his lips to mine, gently at first so that the kiss radiated heat and pleasure from my mouth right around the rest of my body. His hard tongue softly parted my lips and swirled around in my mouth, slowly and politely at first but then probing my own tongue and teeth with what seemed like a very real and increasingly urgent desire. So, I smiled to myself, as I pushed my own tongue against his and tasted the inside of his mouth, this goes to disprove the old saying that whores don't kiss.

'Shall we go?' he enquired. I looked at the clock. It was a quarter to midnight. The function would be ending in fifteen minutes but there was no longer any need to hang around here. As Olivier and I disappeared into the night, I knew that my colleagues would all be talking about Hannah and her amazing new man. But although I'd hired Olivier to impress them, I no longer cared what they thought; right now, all I could think about was the effect he was having on me. As Olivier hailed a taxi in the street I noticed again his long, lean legs, shown off to perfection by that sharply tailored suit. In the back seat of the cab, he kissed me again. Tenderly. Sensitively. And worth every fucking penny.

Oliver paid for the cab, an expense that I supposed would appear on my bill. As we rode the lift up to my flat, he began to take off my dress, sliding the straps over my shoulders and forcing my breasts out of the bra I wore. He held a nipple in each hand, pulling my breasts out so they hung over the top of my dress. As I fumbled for the key in the lock, he stood behind me, a breast in each hand, supporting their weight and then dropping them, fingers lightly pinching each nipple, his face buried in my neck. I felt my legs begin to shake. My panties were now saturated with sweet warm juices and a trickle of moisture escaped and began to roll down the inside of my thigh. I could smell how aroused I was, and I was sure Olivier could, too.

We stepped over the threshold of my apartment and pushed the door closed behind us. He unzipped my dress, removed my bra and rolled my panties down my legs then kneeled before me like a slave to undo each shoe in turn. It was immensely arousing. Before discarding my panties, he held them to his nose and breathed in deeply. Now I was naked apart from my jewellery, which I kept on as a reminder that I was the one paying, a symbol of my real status, power and control. I needed to wear my diamonds because I didn't feel in control at all; I felt at the mercy of this sexy, sophisticated man who knew exactly where a woman needed to be touched.

I watched Olivier disrobe. Confidently, slowly, he peeled off layers of expensive clothing to reveal a toned olive body: my fantasy man from the computer screen made flesh before my eyes. He picked me up in his arms and I felt a sizzle of desire as our bare skin touched for the first time. He carried me into my bedroom, his face buried in my chest, a hardening nipple between his lips, and sat me on the edge of my bed. With one hand inside each thigh, he pushed my legs apart as far as they would go. Then he pushed them a little bit further, so I felt a build-up of a dull tension as my muscles stretched out. I could feel his breath on my waiting pussy for a few seconds before he planted a light, butterfly kiss directly on my clitoris. He hooked my knees over his shoulders, so that my legs remained splayed, and used his fingers to part the skin around my clitoris, leaving it exposed, vulnerable and deliciously sensitive. Next, Olivier went to work with his tongue, tracing tiny shapes on the skin around my clit, teasingly avoiding direct contact with the bud itself. Round, up, down, round, up, down, teasing me and keeping it steady until I cried out. I felt my orgasm build slowly, steadily, a completely different kind of arousal to any I'd felt before.

He carried on working my body like the professional he was. Olivier knew just the right moment to slide a thumb into my pussy, his digit exploring me inside, his tongue never leaving my clitoris. He slid another finger up and then another. The circling of his tongue on my clit turned to sucking and his teeth nipped me right on my clitoris. I squealed and began to buck and writhe. And I was coming, a harder, stronger, longer-lasting orgasm than ever before, overpowering contractions radiating through my entire body. Olivier pulled his fingers away and hardened his tongue and thrust it into my quivering pussy so that it had something to wrap around as the waves of pleasure died down.

As Olivier stood up, I lay down on my front, wincing as my sensitive pudenda brushed against the bedclothes. I was eye level with his hard, upright dick.

'You don't need to,' he said as I extended my tongue and slowly licked the underside of his cock, but his voice was wavering. 'Tonight is about me giving pleasure to you.'

'I need to taste you,' I said, and I meant it; I was possessed by the need to wrap my lips around him. Enthralled, I studied his rod from his black bush to the glossy pink tip. I put my lips together to kiss the tip of it, teasing him, swirling lips and tongue around, daring him to penetrate my mouth. I could feel how excited he was. A drip of clear pre-cum fluid leaked from the tip of his penis and I relished its sharp saltiness. The self-control that Olivier had exhibited all night suddenly evaporated: he began fucking my face. I let him shove his big dick right into my throat, watching his face relax as he abandoned himself to pleasure. Pleasure that I was giving him. I could have stayed sucking that dick all night. The more I sucked, the hotter and wetter my pussy got. I was astonished: after an orgasm as intense as the one I'd just experienced, I thought I'd used up my quota of sexual pleasure for at least a month. But as the tip of Olivier's dick banged hard against the roof of my mouth, I realised that I was ready for round two.

Olivier pulled out his dick from between my lips. I knew he would have come in my mouth if he hadn't. He pushed my body back on the bed, hands on my breasts, before kissing me on the neck again, making my body spasm as a droplet of liquid leaked out from between my legs. As he balanced on his forearms and leaned over me, the light from my jewellery cast tiny brilliant lights on his skin.

He paused for a second to retrieve a condom he'd placed on the chair beside the bed, and I watched him unroll it on to his dick that was bouncing and twitching and growing even bigger by the minute. Then he was inside me, his huge cock filling me up and about to split me in two. He was kissing me, his tongue in my mouth thrusting in and out in time with the vigorous thrusting of his penis. If Olivier was just going through the motions of passion, he was a brilliant actor: I had never felt more desired. With a strong hand, he pulled up my thigh so that it was level with his side. This change in position meant that his dick was rubbing furiously against my clitoris. This is it, I thought as I began to rush and my vision began to blur, it's going to happen, it's going to happen soon.

Pounding and panting, he exploded inside me, pressing down on my exhausted, engorged clit as he did so. We came at the same time, breathing in each other's breath as our bodies pulsated and convulsed, less intense than the first orgasm but longer-lasting. It was the sweetest relief I had ever known. I lay on my back with Olivier on top of me, feeling his spent dick grow limp inside me. After a few moments, he withdrew, got rid of the condom, cleaned himself up, kissed me again.

I looked at my bedside clock. It was 2.30 a.m. Olivier and I had been in my apartment for around an hour. That fuck had cost me five hundred pounds. I got up and reached for my purse, safe in the knowledge that it had been worth every penny. But when I tried to hand a wad of crisp £50 notes to Olivier, he shook his head and refused the money.

'I usually have to pretend,' he said, smiling. 'I usually have to fake it. But that was the best fuck of my life. That one was on the house.'

'Thank you,' I said, flattered and pleased. I watched him dress, savouring my last glimpse of his body before he let himself out of the apartment and hailed a cab in the street. I waved to the taxi, wondering if I'd ever see him again. Probably not: why risk spoiling a perfect memory? And I might never get another fuck on the house. The best things in life are free, after all.

SUCKER PUNCH

Do you believe in love at first sight? No? Well, what about lust? Okay, so what happens when you fall madly in love with someone who you've never even met? Does that count? Can it be real? I would have said a definite no before I heard Carrie's story. You probably won't know who Carrie is, but you will know the man she loved from afar for years: a champion boxer, a household name, she had known he was the man for her from the minute she saw him on television. But would meeting him in the flesh live up to her expectations? Yes. Oh, yes . . .

The first time I saw him I felt like someone had reached a hand deep inside me and pulled all my organs in towards the bottom of my pelvis. Funny little hot and cold pangs I'd never experienced before manifested themselves between my legs. I was only fourteen. I didn't know who he was or what he did. I had no interest in sport of any kind when I saw this beautiful, rugged man in a suit on a sports programme that my dad was watching one Sunday night many years ago. There he was, this man whose body, voice, whose very presence on the screen made me feel so strange I almost fainted. There was something about him I couldn't explain. Of course, I now know that what I was feeling was my first thunderbolt of pure lust, that all I wanted was to have his erect cock in my pussy. But back then, all I could have told you was that there was something special about this man: fifteen years my senior, a world-famous athlete and a perfect stranger. I felt a connection to him. I reckon anyone else watching that night just saw a tough guy, fourteen stones of solid muscle, a nose that had been broken a dozen times, a designer suit and short, dark blond hair. But I saw something different. I saw a vulnerability behind the tough-guy body language, a softness behind the scars.

They say you can't love someone you haven't met but I knew different. Overnight, he became my obsession, my focus in life. I, who had never been interested in any kind of sports before, found out his name and his entire career history, in short, I became an expert on boxing. I read the sports section of my dad's newspaper and spent hours in the library searching the archives for every one of his past fights. Sometimes, when I looked at pictures of him taken in the ring, I'd find that my hand had slipped down the neckline of my top or was between my legs and I'd been touching myself without even realising it. Certain pictures – the ones of him naked but for his shorts, covered in sweat, his blond hair so plastered with sweat that it was almost brown, those blue eyes puffy and swollen – would get me so hot that I would place my thumb on the special place between my legs, squeeze my thighs tightly together and rock back and forth until that warm, liquid feeling engulfed my body. I taped his fights, waited until I was alone in the house and played them back, touching myself as I gazed at his body. I was transfixed by his brute strength, his lumbering grace.

The first time I went to see him fight I was sixteen. I was so excited that I dressed as though for a first date: shaved my legs, had my bikini line waxed for the first time, wore matching underwear, washed and blow-dried my hair. It was ridiculous. I didn't expect to meet him or anything – I wasn't ready for that then, it was enough just to see him in the flesh – but I felt that I had to look my best for him. My parents looked at each other indulgently as we took our places in the second row, content to humour this teenage crush that they thought I would grow out of one day. That fight was the best night of my life so far. When his coach doused him with water at the end of the second round, droplets from the bottle flew on to my face. I sucked my upper lip, tasting water that had been in a bottle pressed to his mouth, convincing myself that this was the next best thing to a kiss.

I never did grow out of this teenage crush. As I grew up, left home and got a job, I followed him around the world, going to every fight I could. I always sat in one of the front few rows, no matter how much it cost me. And I always looked my best for him. Sometimes I'd get to my feet and cheer him on with an enthusiasm that bordered on sexual hysteria, sometimes I'd close my eyes and silently will him to win. The proudest and happiest moments of my life were the ones where his gloved hands were held aloft at the end of the match, when he was presented with belts and trophies.

By the time I was in my early twenties, I noticed that he didn't win as often as he used to. Something was wrong. From my seat in the front row, I could see a few wrinkles in that craggy, broken face, flecks of grey in his short hair. He was still the most masculine and powerful man I'd ever set eyes on. But cracks were starting to show. New scars took longer to heal. I wanted to take him to bed and make slow, tender, healing love to him.

I took lovers in the meantime, of course; some of them teased me about my scrapbooks of newspaper cuttings and of the pictures I kept on my walls. But none of them ever guessed that whenever we fucked I would close my eyes and think of a strong boxer man moving deep inside me. Pretending I was making love to him was the only way I could come through sex.

On the night of his worst defeat I was there as usual, dressed to the nines, hoping that the more effort I made, the stronger he would be. I was twenty-five and he was nearly forty. I had been in love with him for eleven years. It was irrational, but my obsession was now beyond rationality or logic. I was in my usual front-row seat: I had become such a regular fixture over the years that the other die-hard fans, the managers, the agents and the journalists recognised me and we nodded our hellos to each other. I was on the edge of my seat as he made his big entrance, rock music blaring through the speakers. His body was bulky and ripped in red silk shorts, his solid thighs tapering into strong calves in boxing boots, and then there was that torso that had suffered a thousand punches. That body that I had made love to every inch of in my dreams and fantasies.

He fought an American boxer almost half his age, and I watched as my baby took blow after blow after blow. His dignity moved me almost to tears as his glistening body struggled to keep up with his opponent. My fighter was strong but he wasn't as fast or agile as he'd once been. He managed to plant a few killer blows that had me leaping to my feet and cheering him on, but they were not enough. He just didn't see the young man's punches coming.

The fight was over in less than three minutes. I saw

him take a blow to the cheek and sway for a few seconds before collapsing to the floor. It was heartbreaking, like watching a giant oak tree felled by a gale. Blood and saliva flew through the air and landed on the mat. I leapt to my feet, silently willing him to wake up, be strong, fight again, but he stayed where he was, not coming round until the eleventh second. When he opened his blue eyes they were glassy and unfocused. He blinked as the photographers' flashbulbs popped around his face. For a split-second we made eye contact, and I thought I understood his unspoken message: it's time for all this attention, this madness to end. To finally hold his gaze sent a thrill of desire down my spine and directly to my clitoris, but my desire was diminished by the fact that my heart was breaking for him.

My reverie was broken as men in suits clambered through the ropes, wrapped him in a red silk robe and spirited him away from me. I sat glumly down in my seat, listening to reporters and fans all around me saying that it was over, that his career had finished. The journalists seemed to be thinking up witty headlines whilst traipsing out to the victor's press conference. I simmered with rage at their lack of respect. Any normal fan would accept that it came with the territory, but I wasn't capable of such objectivity. And normal boxing fans aren't mentally and physically infatuated with the boxer.

I was in no mood to press myself against all those bodies and endure the crush as the stadium emptied, still less to queue for hours for the exit in my car. I sat in my seat until the auditorium was empty, staring at the deserted boxing ring. When I was sure I had the place to myself, I crept up to the ropes, beyond them my darling's towel lay on the mat in a crumpled heap. I reached in and picked it up, held it to my nose and shook with excitement to know that I was breathing in his actual essence for the first time. It smelled meaty and masculine and made my pussy swell alarmingly quickly. God, I was definitely taking this as a souvenir: in my car I would part my legs and rub this towel frantically between my thighs until the friction on my clit brought me to orgasm and relieved the tension. The closest we would ever come to making love, to fucking.

His agent, looking downcast, wandered over to me.

'Hello you,' he said. We weren't on first-name terms but he'd seen me often enough to recognise me. 'What are you still doing here? Waiting for someone?' How could I tell him that there was only one someone for me, and that it was his client?

'Just feeling a bit low after the fight,' I said. 'I thought I'd give the crowds a while to disperse before I went home.'

'He's a broken man,' admitted his agent. 'This was his big fight. Between you and me, don't be surprised if he retires soon.'

All the blood in my body rushed away from my clit and started pounding in my chest. He couldn't retire, where would I go to see him? What would I do? I slumped back in my seat again, the towel wrapped around my neck.

'Maybe you could cheer him up,' suggested the agent.

'Me?' I said, not quite believing what I had heard.

'Yeah. He's in despair back there. I can't get through to him. Maybe his number one fan could reassure him.'

I shook with desire and anticipation as I followed the agent down a series of breeze block corridors. My heels echoed on the vinyl floor as we walked under stark strip lighting, past fire exits and security doors. Not a romantic atmosphere to most, but it was to me; these were the corridors and tunnels that he would walk on his way to and from a fight. Finally we stopped at a red door, the same colour as his shorts. I felt panic flutter in my ribcage and desire pluck at my pussy. Maybe it was a mistake to meet him. What if my fantasy man, my broken boxer, let me down in reality? But it was too late now.

'Someone to see you,' the agent said, rapping on the door.

'Another journalist come to get the exclusive on my big failure?' snapped a gruff voice from inside.

'No, no.' said the agent. 'I'll let her introduce herself.'

Then he turned to me. 'I'm going to the press conference. Be back in an hour or so.'

I put my fingers on the door handle and opened the door. He was a lonely figure slumped on a chair in the corner of his dressing room, bottle of water in a hand covered in the bandages he wore under his boxing glove and still in his shorts, robe and boots. His craggy cheek was fast turning a rainbow of yellow and violet colours and the blood was starting to dry on his cheek. The sharp tang of fresh sweat, imbued with his own personal aroma, filled the room. Now that I was so close to him I didn't have a clue what to say. I was unprepared for the way my body would react when it met him in the flesh. Now that I was near enough to touch him and could smell his rugged masculine aroma, years of sexual fantasy and obsession were suddenly pounding through my flesh, lifting me up and making my pussy pump like a piston and my head swim.

'It's you!' he said, looking surprised.

'You know who I am?' I replied, stunned.

'I've noticed you. I always assumed you were someone's wife or girlfriend. Women as beautiful as you are only at matches on the arm of their rich husbands. It's unusual for a woman to come and see a fight on her own.'

'Well, I do,' I replied. 'Only for you.'

'I see,' he said. 'I'm very flattered. After tonight's match

I thought that nothing good would come of today but you may have just saved it!' He tried to smile but his mangled face winced at the movement.

'Oh!' I said. It was horrible to see him in such pain. 'Let me clean that up for you.'

Glad I could do something to help him, I grabbed some cotton wool from the dressing table and walked to the sink that stood in the corner of the room, running cold water over the wool. I drew closer to him, spread my legs so that I had one thigh either side of his lap and his head was level with my breasts. I was so close to him that the heat from his body made mine even warmer and I could see every tiny scar on his face. My whole body was singing and tingling and I was sure he'd hear how fast my pulse raced. My cunt hovered just a few inches away from his naked, sweaty, glistening torso. His cornflower-blue eyes looked up into mine.

'Be gentle with me,' he joked. 'I couldn't take another blow tonight.'

I didn't reply but instead bathed his wound with cotton wool, cleaning the blood and the sweat from his broken, swollen skin. The injury beneath wasn't all that bad. I cleaned him up as tenderly as I'd ever touched anyone. I stroked his hair, told my fighter it was all going to be okay, soothed him. Without thinking what I was doing, I pulled his head towards me and cradled it in between my breasts. I had meant it as a comforting, non-sexual gesture but his soft damp cheek on my cleavage sent a jolt of arousal through me that made me gasp. Over the locker-room smell of his dressing room, I could detect another, musky scent: my own juices beginning to ooze out of my pussy. If I could smell it, surely he could, too.

I rocked him back and forth. He nuzzled his head deeper and deeper into my cleavage and when he lifted a bandaged hand to my top, pulled down a strap to expose my breast and put his lips gently to my nipple, it seemed like the only course of action he could have taken. I tipped my head back, closed my eyes and abandoned my body to the delicious release of sexual tension that had built up for over a decade. I leaned in towards him and kissed his battered cheek, followed by our first mouth-to-mouth kiss, a soft, salty affair that lasted for an eternity and made small talk redundant. The hands that I knew could knock a man out with one blow were gentle on my breasts, my thighs, my belly, as he slowly caressed and explored my body. I felt soft and vulnerable next to him, and the roughness of the bandages that still bound his knuckles created an arousing friction on my own soft skin.

He pulled away. 'I'm a mess.' he mumbled. 'Do you want me to shower?'

I shook my head. 'I want you fresh from the fight,' I whispered, and placed my hand between his legs. My fingers closed on soft balls which raised up as I cupped them, and then on a hard, erect shaft which I stroked through the silk of his shorts before pulling out his waistband and releasing his quivering hard-on. It was a perfect match for the rest of his body, thick, stout and strong. He pulled my panties to one side and began to gently stroke my clitoris, my juices seeping on to his bandaged hands. He slid one finger inside me and my greedy hole closed around it. His face was buried in the crevice of my breasts, and my nipples were swollen as he took first one, then the other, between his tongue and lips and sucked gently again. The softer his tongue, the hotter and wetter my pussy got. I always knew that my gentle giant would reserve his tenderest touches for me.

I lowered myself down his body, my pussy and bush tickling the length of his chest from his pecs to his rock-hard stomach until I was positioned just over his dick. Shifting around until I felt the tip of it, I lowered myself down on it gently, gently, slowly feeling his warmth and bulk fill me up and stretch my insides. I was aware of the size of his thighs between my legs, of the bulging biceps that flexed and rippled every time his arms moved to hold my waist or grab my arse. I grabbed on to his shoulders, twisted and ground my hips, enjoying the way I was hugging him, massaging his prick deep inside me. He used all his considerable strength to push his hips up towards my body, forcing himself deeper inside me, deeper than any man had ever been before. He placed one chunky fingertip on my clitoris and pressed down gently. I came, my cunt turned to liquid, ripples of pleasure that felt as if they would never end. Nor did I want them to. As my pussy closed around his dick, he shot his load inside me. I relaxed my legs, then wrapped them around his back, tilted my face up for another kiss. We stayed like this, holding each other close, while his dick contracted and his spunk spilled from my slit, staining his silk shorts. I kissed the top of his head and stroked his hair.

'So,' I said to him, half-afraid of the answer. 'Are you really going to retire? Because if you do, I don't know what I'm going to do with my life.'

He placed a kiss on my right nipple. 'I honestly don't know,' he replied. 'But either way, you'll be fine.'

I didn't understand.

'If I retire, I will have to take you away and marry you so that I can spend the rest of my life fucking you. And if I don't, you will have to be my lucky charm and follow me round the world, watching me fight until can't fight any more. Will you stick around?'

He knew that the answer would be yes.

And that's the story of how my fighter, my lover, my husband, kept on fighting, kept travelling the world and became the oldest world heavyweight champion of all time.

The day he won back his title we made love on the floor of the boxing ring. He hasn't lost a fight since. As long as he has me by his side he'll never be defeated again. And he will always, always have me.

ALWAYS THE
BRIDESMAID

Our same-sex fantasies often involve celebrities, colleagues or casual acquaintances. But sometimes we find that a little sapphic experimentation happens closer to home. Sometimes, we suddenly see friends we've known for a lifetime in a whole new light. That's what happened to Polly . . .

'Oh my God, Polly!' shrieked Sammy we turned the key and entered the honeymoon suite of the Park Court hotel. 'This place is AMAZING!'

I looked around at the four-poster bed dressed in white linen and scattered with rose petals, the floor-to-ceiling Venetian mirrors and the roll-top bath on a platform in one corner of the room. Sammy was right. It was amazing.

'It's lush, isn't it?' I said, turning to my best friend and bridesmaid. 'It's almost a shame to share it with you.' I winked so she'd know I was joking. Sammy was spending my last night of singledom with me, keeping me prisoner in my bedroom, so that I wouldn't run the risk of seeing Steve, my fiancé, the night before the wedding.

He was in the same hotel but sequestered away in another wing with his friends. Steve and I had made a pact that he could have the bar while Sammy and I would stay in my room, pampering ourselves with the most luxurious and expensive room service available.

As soon as we'd unpacked our bags and I'd hung my wedding dress on the back of the wardrobe door, Sammy ran to the minibar. 'Look at these!' she said, holding up two small champagne bottles. 'Aren't they cute?'

I was busy checking out all the posh products in the bathroom. 'Look at *this*!' I said, surveying a large beauty hamper with rows of luxury shampoos, conditioners, massage oils and face packs. 'We've got our own personal spa tucked in here! There's enough lotions and potions to keep us busy all evening.'

'Not that you need it, Polly,' said Sammy, her eyes shining. 'You've never looked more beautiful than you do tonight.' I was touched by her compliment. I'd been dieting, working out, looking after myself in the run-up to my big day, and it's nice to feel appreciated. I'd also had long, blonde hair extensions, making me feel like my fantasy woman, a princess: a fairy-tale hairstyle for my fairytale day. 'Seriously,' she said, stroking a strand of platinum hair that fell across my shoulders. 'Steve's a lucky, lucky man.'

'Thanks,' I said, flattered. 'You're not so bad yourself.' And it was true. Since she'd met Jez, her boyfriend, Sammy had blossomed. Dark and slender where I was blonde and curvy, she had recently grown more confident and beautiful than ever.

'But you never can be *too* pretty,' I said, surveying the beauty products. 'I don't know where to start!'

'I do,' said Sammy, cracking open a mini champagne bottle and handing it to me. Good idea, girl, I thought, feeling very glad that Sam was my chief bridesmaid.

After finishing our drinks, we took it in turns to shower using the luxurious sugar and olive oil body scrubs in the bathroom. Then we both slipped into white hotel dressing gowns, commenting on how soft our skin felt under the fluffy towelling. Next we applied face packs which were supposed to set but didn't, because we couldn't stop talking. We tried to give each other pedicures using the foot scrubs and peppermint lotions in the bathroom, but kept tickling each other so much that we didn't get very far. Still determined to take full advantage of the free products, Sammy rummaged further into the beauty hamper.

'What about this?' she asked, holding up a bottle of massage oil. 'Want a nice relaxing massage?' I didn't know the first thing about massage and neither did Sammy, but we were determined to get value for money out of these body treatments.

'Sure,' I said. 'I'll do you first. Where's tense?'

'Backs of my legs,' she said. 'I've spent too long on that bloody step machine trying to get in shape for tomorrow's dress. My thighs might not be wobbly, but they sure are stiff.' Sammy lay face down on the bed and hitched up her robe so that the tops of her thighs and the bottom of her arse were exposed. Her bottom was as soft as a peach, and her thighs were lean and slender. I poured a little massage oil on to the smooth skin and using gentle kneading motions began to massage her.

'Ooh, that's lovely,' purred Sammy. 'You're very good. Just there,' she said, as my knuckles worked the crease where her bottom met her legs. I used the flat of my palms to smooth the oil deep into her skin, and following her instructions about what felt good, my hands swirled around her butt cheeks. Only when I found my thumbs drifting towards Sammy's inner thighs did I realise that my massage might be about to get a little too intimate. I'd been so focused on how good her baby-soft skin felt beneath my palms, and her moans of pleasure, I'd forgotten that there are some places you just don't touch your friends.

'Right,' I said, ending my massage session with some brisk, efficient strokes somewhere near Sammy's knees. 'I'm done now.'

'That was bliss,' said Sammy, rolling over on to her back. Her face was flushed, and as she turned over, her robe became unfastened, revealing a small, pert breast topped with a soft, puffy nipple. She pulled her gown back towards her chest within seconds, but I'd seen something that made me feel nervous and uneasy.

'Your turn now,' she said, and as she spoke I noticed that she didn't look me in the eye. 'Tell me where your aches and pains are.'

I moaned about how much my shoulders ached after weeks of poring over menus and seating plans and orders of service and Sammy said she would do her best to get rid of the tension. I lay on my front, tits slightly splayed to the sides, and slid the top of my robe off, but kept it tied around my waist, covering my arse. When Sammy poured the massage oil on to my back, it trickled and tickled deliciously. Her hands on my neck and shoulders were warm, slender and strong; I was impressed by the way she found each knot of tension and released it with masterful strokes as though she had been doing this her whole life. And I could tell that she was enjoying it too, as she responded to the feedback I gave her and even complimented me on my all-over tan.

The more confident she grew, the further her hands travelled: her sensitive caresses worked their way down my arms, releasing all the tension I carried around in my hands, and her fingers slid under my arms, teasingly touching the sides of my breasts. If Sammy had been a boy, this would be the most effective foreplay ever! I decided to remind myself to joke with her later about teaching Steve a thing or two.

'Okay,' said Sammy eventually, when I was just about to drift off to sleep. 'You're done. How did that feel?'

'Amazing,' I said, and meant it. I sat up, pulling my robe back on and sinking into the pillows. 'So now what?'

'Well,' said Sammy, surveying the room. 'I think we've used up just about everything in here, so now it's time to take advantage of the room service.'

We ordered champagne and oysters which arrived on a silver tray. I'd never had oysters before, and Sammy showed me how to eat them, putting the shell to my lips and tipping my head back so that they slid down my throat. 'Just let it glide down,' she advised. 'A bit like swallowing after a blow job.'

When Sammy ate oysters, she looked elegant and sexy whereas I failed the first couple of attempts and got more shellfish up my nose than into my mouth. Sammy leaned over and helped me out; putting her hand under my chin, she tenderly tipped my head back at the right angle and I swallowed the delicate muscle and liquor down whole. When I finally did it properly, I was instantly hooked on the salty, slippery sexiness of oysters. I made a mental note to order some of these when Steve and I were on our honeymoon.

Our next course was a steak dinner, washed down with gorgeous red wine, followed by a fresh fruit salad drowned in whipped cream which Sammy and I fed to each other with our fingers. Stuffed and happy, we retired to the bed where we sat cross-legged, drinking a little more wine and talking about the future, reminiscing about the past.

At around midnight, I felt my eyelids begin to get heavy. 'I think that just about does me for tonight. I'm tired,' I said. 'Mind if we go to sleep? If ever there was a night I needed my beauty sleep, it's tonight.'

We both brushed our teeth and changed into our night things. Sammy wore a vest-and-shorts set that showed off her slender, boyish figure to perfection. I debuted the negligee that I had been saving for my wedding night but which was so beautiful I couldn't resist wearing it. It was made of white silk with a lace trim that scooped up my breasts up and pushed them together, giving me a full, round cleavage. If you looked closely (which I hoped Steve would) you could see the outline of my pink nipples through the sheer fabric.

Sammy gave me a wolf-whistle when she saw me. 'Here comes the bride!' she said from her side of the four-poster bed. 'That's beautiful. Steve won't be able to resist you.'

I turned out the light, but neither of us could sleep,

too excited about the day that lay ahead of us. So we talked some more. Gradually the conversation turned around to sex, like it always does when two female friends chat for long enough.

'I think it's so beautiful what you're doing,' Sammy said wistfully. 'I don't know if I could make that kind of commitment.'

'But you and Jez are rock solid,' I said.

'Oh, I know that,' she replied. 'There's just so much I want to do, I'm not sure if you can do it with just one person.'

'Like what?' I said, curious.

'I don't know. Just stuff. I haven't experimented that much, and maybe I should. Like, I've never been with a woman, I've never had a threesome, I've never let anyone go up my bum . . .' I started giggling, suddenly aware of Sammy's warm presence in the bed beside me. I became uncomfortable and excited as vivid visions of my best friend doing all these things ran through my mind before I could stop them.

'Have *you* ever?' she said, in a too-loud voice that was probably meant to sound casual. In fact, it sounded anything but. 'Been with a woman, I mean?'

'You know I haven't!' I laughed. 'I'd have told you if I had!'

'But have you thought about it?' said Sammy. She

wasn't going to let this topic go. 'Have you fantasised about it? I have. I have the most explicit dreams about fucking women. Ones I know. Sometimes my dreams are so horny that I wake up and I'm actually coming. Don't you have dreams like that?'

'Well . . . yes . . .' I replied, wondering exactly which women Sammy had fantasised about being with. 'Thinking about it, or watching it, or reading about it can be quite horny. But there's a difference between thinking something and actually doing it. Some fantasies are better left as just that. What if the real thing isn't as hot as you'd like it to be?'

'Oh, I think it would be,' said Sammy. 'In fact, I think it'd be pretty fucking amazing. Even talking about it with you is getting me turned on right now.'

An abrupt, awkward silence ensued as I digested Sammy's words. I could tell by her absolute stillness and her controlled breathing that she wasn't asleep, and as I looked at the clock which said 1 a.m., I had never felt more awake in my entire life. I was thinking about how her peachy arse had looked when I was massaging her that evening, how smooth, soft and lightly tanned the skin. I thought of how her slender body had felt between my thighs when I received her massage. But more than this, the picture that replayed itself in my head, again and again, like a broken DVD continually tracking back over the same scene, was the moment when she'd rolled over and exposed that flash of breast. I'd seen Sammy's tits a hundred times over the years: we'd shared changing rooms and of course beds before now. But that glimpse, that stolen glance at her flesh, had been different. Private. Arousing. And now she'd confessed that she was up for a girl-on-girl experience, and that she was horny, actively horny, this minute. And she was so close I could feel the tiny hairs on her arms brush against my skin. Arms that I suddenly realised I wanted to reach out and pull me close, hands that I wanted to explore my thighs, my belly, my breasts, my pussy.

I let out a gasp of astonishment and desire and Sammy rolled over to face me. The only light in the room came from the moonlight through the curtains, and I could see her slim hips and the curve of her shoulder outlined underneath the thin sheets.

'Polly,' she said in a low, cracked whisper. 'Are you awake?'

I said yes. The noise came out like a kind of strangled moan, the unmistakable sound of someone madly turned on and struggling to control it.

'Can't you sleep either?' she said, shifting a little bit closer to me. As I felt her soft breath caress my bare arms and neck, I realised I was in trouble. Mild curiosity had turned into desire that was snowballing out of control.

My own breath came in short, sharp rasps and I felt my breasts rise and fall rapidly, the lace bodice scratching my soft skin, making my nipples swell and harden.

'Poll,' said Sammy, in that same husky whisper. 'Can I touch you?'

Without waiting for an answer, she extended a slim, white hand and placed it on my breast, thumb and fore-finger gripping my nipple through the lace. Her soft pinch caused my pussy to squeeze and flutter and I knew that soon I would be wet. I lay frozen still for a couple of seconds, knowing that if I wanted to stop this, I had to do so now. But my body betrayed me and I let out an involuntary moan that told Sammy just how good her hands felt. She slid her hand under the lace, warm fingers cupping my breast, then kneading it, her other hand pulling down the lace straps of my negligee so that both my tits were exposed. In the half-light I saw her rise up and she placed her knees either side of my body, pinning me to the bed. She went to work on my tits, touching and massaging them with the same tenderness she'd applied to my back and shoulders a few hours earlier, but this time she wasn't getting rid of tension, she was building it up. My body began to coil like a tight spring.

As she bent down to kiss me, I lifted my head up to meet hers. There in the dark, we found each other's lips, her soft velvet mouth brushing my own gently at first, then her tongue sliding in between my teeth while I kissed back with ever-increasing passion.

My hands stretched up to her breasts then, feeling her soft, bulbous nipples through the thin jersey of her vest. I placed one hand on each of her small breasts, enjoying the way the firm flesh yielded to my fingers. Sammy let out a tiny whimper which made me want to do more than just touch her tits. I wriggled out from under Sammy's legs, hoisted myself up so that we were kneeling on the bed, face to face.

'This is so horny,' said Sammy, as we knelt there with our arms around each other, kissing passionately. She stroked my hair, then tentatively reached down for the hem of my negligee. Eagerly I raised my arms in the air as she slid the flimsy dress off my body as gently as though it were a feather. I was naked now, my hair tickling my shoulders, my tits level with Sammy's. I needed to feel our nipples rubbing together and hurriedly I tore off her vest, whipping it over her head and throwing it across the room. Pulling her towards me again by the waistband of her shorts, I kissed her: our tits were finally touching, her puffy little nipples teasing and tickling my own which tingled and expanded in response.

I bent my head and pressed my lips to her perfect, perky breasts, so different to my full, round globes. I kissed the dark rosy nipple, gently sucked it for a few seconds, enjoying the way her flesh was trapped and squeezed between my lips. Then I had her whole breast in my mouth, licking the underside, sucking the nipple. While my lips and tongue treated Sammy's right breast to soft, tender caresses, my hand was greedily grabbing and kneading her left. This contrast of hard and soft was driving her wild: I could tell by the way she trembled and moaned.

We pulled apart, both of us breathing heavily. Sammy placed my hand on her hips. I read her unspoken command and began to tug at her shorts, pulling them down to her knees. Briefly, she was on all fours, and I reached out and pulled the shorts off over her ankles, flinging them across the room. She rose to face me again, her bush and mine were level: I could feel a swelling and a dampness between my legs and a sweet, sexy smell that wasn't my own filled my nostrils – Sammy's body was responding just the way mine was. Our tits and pussies and lips crashed into each other.

Instinctively, I put my knee between Sammy's legs, forcing her thighs to part a little. Now we were both kneeling with our legs apart. When she reached her hand between my legs and tentatively touched my clitoris, I felt a fresh wave of white-hot pleasure sweep over me. With two fingers, she stroked it delicately. I returned the compliment, sliding my fingers between her dewy thighs.

First of all I felt her pussy lips, damp, swollen and slippery. There was no mistaking her clitoris, a hot little bud of flesh protruding from between her legs. Softly, so gently, I brushed it with the back of my knuckle and felt Sammy's legs begin to tremble. Working in rhythm with each other, we began to rub each others clits, slowly at first, increasing pressure and tempo as we became more and more excited. Sammy rocked backwards and forwards on her knees, chanting my name in my ear again and again in a guttural whisper that hardly sounded like her at all.

'Oh, Polly,' she rasped. 'Oh, fuck, baby, oh, Polly, that's so good.' Her own hand was deep inside me now, her fingers curved, beckoning to a secret, delicious area deep inside my cunt, the inside of her wrist bashing crudely against my twitching clitoris.

The more she spoke, the faster I rubbed her until my hand was dripping with her sweet juices. Her pussy contracted once, then twice, then went into spasm, a quick succession of blissful little squeezes as she succumbed to her orgasm.

'Oh Poll, oh dear God, I'm gonna come, I'm gonna come, oh, you dirty little, aaaaaaaaaaaaaaaah.' I clamped my lips down on Sammy's nipple as she came, licking the beads of sweat off her chest, feeling the searing heat of orgasm as it ripped through her body.

Sammy didn't allow herself any recovery time and she

didn't stop. Her hand continued to twist inside me, her penetrating fingers more sensitive, nimble and deft than any man's dick could ever be. With a final flick, I came too, feeling my pussy hug Sammy's hand. A final gush of sweet liquid squirted out of me and trailed down the inside of her arm. She held still until the final, gentle aftershocks of my climax had subsided, then withdrew her hand and held it to my nose. I did the same: we stayed like that for a while, each smelling the musk of our own pussy on the other's hand. Finally, exhausted and satisfied, we slept, both of us naked, not bothering to pull the covers over our bodies, clinging to each other for warmth.

We woke up at 8 a.m. to the sound of my mother knocking on the door. The room, so dark and sexy the night before, was now flooded with sunlight. Sammy and I looked at each other and stifled giggles as we dashed around the room, trying to locate the nightclothes we'd peeled from each other just seven hours ago. By the time I opened the door to my mother, the room was tidy and we were both respectably dressed in hotel bathrobes.

My mother entered the room and studied our faces.

'Well,' she said. 'I had worried that you two would be up all night. But you both look very fresh. You obviously got an early night and plenty of beauty sleep.'

At this, Sammy and I collapsed into giggles. My mum

still doesn't know why we found this so funny, and Steve still doesn't know the secret of my glowing complexion on the big day.

And only Sammy spotted, months later, when we were looking over the wedding photographs, a tiny round love-bite over my left breast, just visible in my low-cut wedding dress. No one else has noticed. And no one else needs to know.

THE MISTRESS'S APPRENTICE

When it comes to sex and power, everyone has a preference. Some women love to be dominated; others love to be the one in control. Finding out whether top or bottom flicks your switch is simply a matter of being in the right place at the right time.

Tina didn't know how thrilling a little power could be until she found herself working in a place where submission and domination were all in a day's work. But how could she take those fantasies about control and turn them into reality?

Cleaning isn't everyone's idea of a dream job, but I love it. I'm my own boss, the money is surprisingly good, and I get real satisfaction from turning messy homes and offices into gleaming perfection. And I like chatting to my clients: I get to meet the ones who arrive early to work in the morning, or stay very late at night. These lonely workaholics are always glad to have someone to talk to and are often surprised that their cleaner is not only pretty but clever too. They're only too grateful for someone to disrupt the boredom and isolation of working on their own in faceless, sterile offices. It does me good to make conversation too. All those grey workplaces, with their plastic plants and photocopier-ink fumes look the same after a while.

All except one. Charlotte's workplace was a little different from the others. Unconventional. Extreme. Just like the woman herself. The woman I wanted to become. Charlotte was my favourite client. She was a smart, glamorous woman in her forties. From the outside, her office looked like any other respectable small business, with its frosted-glass doors, its sleek reception area with a laptop and telephone on the blond wood desk and comfortable sofas for clients to sink into. But inside, on the lower floor, it was a different story. Descend the spiral staircase to the basement, walk through a steel security door and you entered another world. It was a vast cellar, divided into two rooms. One featured exposed brickwork and a concrete floor painted black. The only light came from candles in sconces on the walls. There were hooks for manacles and a stretching rack and a huge mirror. Masks, whips, costumes and sex toys were in custom-made racks and shelves, and there was a vast iron bed-frame with a PVC-covered mattress in one corner. The other room was smaller, a dark chamber covered in black tiling and dominated by an industrial hose and a huge glass bathtub.

Although Charlotte arrived and left work wearing a suit, carrying a briefcase and drove away in a Porsche, she was not your average career girl. She was a talented, experienced and very expensive dominatrix.

I learned about this particular job at one of the big city offices I already cleaned. A rich and powerful American called Howie was a financier and worked until 9 p.m. most nights. We'd struck up a friendship and one day Howie said that I seemed pretty open-minded, and would I be interested earning some extra money working for his 'business contact' Charlotte?

My first interview with Charlotte took place in her upstairs office. I gave her a list of references and started to tell her all about my skills and experience but she seemed more interested in finding out what sort of person I was. She kept asking me if I was discreet. I told her that I often had to tidy up top-secret company documents and contracts worth thousands of pounds but she smiled a funny little smile and said that wasn't quite what she had in mind. Then she beckoned me towards her with a red-taloned finger and I followed her down the spiral staircase, through the steel door and into the dungeon.

'This is where I work,' she said, studying my face for a reaction. 'This is what I do. Men, and some women, pay me to humiliate and abuse them. It can get quite dark, and quite loud, and it's often pretty messy.'

I wasn't shocked: in fact I was thrilled as I pictured the scene: rich businessmen cowering naked on the floor as Charlotte shouted and spat at them. I imagined her in a leather outfit, brandishing her whip, and felt a rush of exhilaration and envy. Far from being shocked, I felt good. Better than ever, in fact. Like I had come home.

'I clean up right after the clients but every night we need to disinfect the whole place, floor to ceiling, just to be safe,' said Charlotte, as casually as though she were telling me where the tea and coffee were kept. 'And you need to keep my sex toys clean, polish the leather and the PVC, make sure all the whips and other bits of kit are just where I need them. Things can get a little crazy down here and I need to know the precise location of everything.'

I nodded, confident that I could do all this. I would take great pleasure in keeping the tools of Charlotte's trade in their current, beautiful condition. It would be a point of pride. I said this to my prospective employer and her crimson lips parted into a smile, revealing dazzling white teeth.

'I like you,' she said, beaming. 'Very much. Will you take the job?'

'I'd love to!' I replied.

'Fabulous,' she said. 'When can you start?'

The very next evening, I found myself in the cool cellar cleaning and tidying. I was slightly disappointed not to see any of Charlotte's clients, curious to know what sort of person paid for her services. My blood ran hot as I thought of an uptight Mr Moneybags type – rather like Howie, in fact – and how he would look, quivering and naked on the floor, whimpering under the dominatrix's whip. And how outrageously horny it would feel to be the woman wielding it. I shivered and tried to concentrate on the job in hand.

The next evening I found a handwritten note from Charlotte thanking me for doing such a great job. I felt a surge of pride and happiness. It felt entirely natural to me to come from cleaning offices to scrubbing down whips and chains in a dungeon but I grew to like it. Over the next few weeks I settled into a routine: I'd let my imagination drift off while I worked, picture myself in the clothes that I washed, imagine it was me in Charlotte's position. I saw her once or twice a week and we'd sit down to enjoy a cup of coffee together. She always wanted to know what I'd been up to and we'd talk about books I'd read, dates I'd been on, that kind of thing. But I never saw any of her clients.

'I take care to book time with my clients when you're not around,' she said. 'They like the anonymity that I give them, and besides, it can sound quite extreme when you're not used to it. You're the best cleaner I've ever had. I'd hate to scare you away.'

I didn't tell her that far from scaring me away, it would probably be all she could do to stop me joining in.

I'd been working for Charlotte for about a month when I came to work one evening to find her dressed in a black and red leather bodysuit, looking beautiful, powerful and sexy but also rather flustered.

'I'm sorry, Tina,' she said. 'I've had to rearrange a booking. There's so much work coming my way these days that I can't really turn it down. I'll be working in the water-torture room while you clean out the dungeon. I can't avoid it. I hope it doesn't disturb you, and do be discreet.'

I nodded and assured her that of course I would. I went about my usual cleaning routine and for a while I heard nothing but the trickle of running water from the wet room and two low, murmuring voices. After a few minutes, curiosity got the better of me and I stopped my cleaning routine, sidled over to the door that divided the two rooms and peered through the keyhole.

I was astonished to find that what I saw turned me on, and quickly. I went, in the split second it took for my eyes to adapt to the murky light in the wet room, from a normal state of being to one of desperate, ravenous sexual hunger. I saw the back view of Charlotte, sexy and strong in her leather costume. Instead of a whip in her hand, she brandished a hose on full power. Charlotte was directing a forceful jet of water at a beautiful young woman, who was strung up against the wall with her hands in manacles, and her legs forced apart by a pair of leg irons. Charlotte was taking it in turns to blast the girl's tits and clit with water. When she trained the hose on her breasts, the flesh dented as though poked by an invisible finger and the woman's nipples, flushed dark brown and highly erect, moved in a series of jiggled, jerky movements. Just when I thought she couldn't take any more, Charlotte would direct the gushing jet against the girl's clit. I watched, crazy with arousal, as the water pummelled the girl's pussy and thighs.

'Oh, mistress, this hurts so good,' she begged. 'Please let me come! Please let me come!'

Charlotte momentarily turned off the jet of water.

'What have I told you about begging me like that?' she said in a stern voice I had never heard her use before.

'I'm sorry,' said the girl, her wet hair slapping at her pink breasts as she hung her head in shame. 'I just need to come so bad.'

'You'll come when I say so, you little bitch,' said Charlotte, and turned the hose back on. She trained it right back on the girl's clitoris: even from where I crouched I could see her pinky-brown pussy convulse a couple of times and her body, constrained by the iron shackles, stiffen then grew limp as she surrendered to her orgasm.

I squeezed my thighs together and rocked back and forth once: that tiny movement was all it took for me to come too, harder and faster than anything I'd ever known. The whole thing from first sight to arousal to orgasm had taken about twenty seconds. I hadn't even had time to get wet, although my post-orgasmic juices were now filling my jeans with a warm dampness. I pressed my sizzling cheek against the cool of the dungeon wall for a few seconds, then drew away from the door.

Somehow I managed to compose myself and complete cleaning the dungeon in record time so that when Charlotte and her client emerged from the wet room, I was upstairs, polishing a desk in the office. I watched as the client, now fresh-faced in a pink tracksuit with her wet hair piled on top of her head, handed Charlotte £500 in cash. She kissed her on the cheek, thanked her and said she was looking forward to seeing her at the same time next week.

'Well,' said Charlotte, counting the money into the safe deposit. 'You've seen what I do now. Are you shocked? Can you handle it?'

So she'd noticed! I feared I'd broken protocol somehow, but she seemed more amused then angry. I nodded my head and then went downstairs to clean out the wet room. Not only could I handle it, I loved it. And I couldn't wait until I saw it happen again.

The next few weeks saw a marked upturn in business for Charlotte, and I'd often find that she had clients in one room while I was cleaning the other. I became expert at tucking myself away so that the clients wouldn't see me. If they did, they'd see me in the reception area for the briefest second, and I wouldn't make eye contact. But I'd seen it all: my work at Charlotte's had become the highlight of my day, my addiction. I needed to get my fix. Whenever I knew she had a client in the basement I'd sneak downstairs, crouch by the door, sometimes using my fingers but more often just pressing my thighs together and rocking until I came. I learned to control my orgasm so that I could come in absolute silence. My bottom lip had a permanent scar on it from where I'd bitten down hard to stop the moans coming out.

One evening I took my position at the door and saw Howie, naked but for a dog leash around his neck, kissing and licking Charlotte's boots. I had always suspected he was a client . . . 'business contact' – yeah *right*. The sight of this guy (whose body was surprisingly buff now that he was out of that starchy suit) who made deals worth thousands of pounds on a daily basis, naked and totally broken like this was the horniest thing I'd ever seen in my life. I bit down so hard on my lip that I broke the skin, tasting my own blood as I pressed my legs together and squeezed, letting the seam of my jeans rub against my clitoris and bring me to orgasm.

After Charlotte went home that night and I was wiping down the clothes she'd worn that day, I decided to play a little dress-up. I slipped off my jeans and T-shirt and put on a red basque and a pair of the Perspex stilettos that Charlotte often wore to walk up and down her clients' spines. I stood before the mirror, loving the woman I became in this outfit. I took a cat o' nine tails down from the wall, wielded it at my reflection. One day, I thought, I will flaunt this whip for real, I will find someone who takes one look at me and turns into a quivering lump of submissive desire, and I will torture that person and make them come harder than they ever have before, and when it's all over, I'm gonna come too, and it will be the most intense, amazing thing I'll ever do in my life. I took the whip between my legs, rubbed the length of the handle along my gusset, let it caress my pounding pussy, and watched my face remain utterly expressionless as I had my second orgasm of the night. Only my cheeks, flushed a deep red, gave any clue to the state of arousal I'd just experienced.

After that night I would sneak into Charlotte's wardrobe and dress up in her clothes whenever I got the chance. I grew bolder and more imaginative and soon began to bark orders at imaginary slaves.

'Kneel before me, you pathetic little prick,' I'd snarl at some fantasy man, picturing a grown male, helpless before me, his erect cock twitching and growing even as I belittled him. I taught myself how to control the whip perfectly, practised locking and unlocking the manacles so that I could do them in double-quick time. When I was cleaning down the wet room, I imagined that the high-powered pressure hose was pointed at bodies, not simply washing detergent off the wall. I got so addicted that I would start to arrive early for my shifts to steal five minutes when I knew that Charlotte wasn't going to be there. I was careful to put everything back exactly where it belonged. I was glad of my professionalism: my system was so fool-proof that Charlotte would never see anything out of place, never guess what I got up to when her back was turned. It had to end, of course. I was taking more and more chances, spending longer and longer in Charlotte's clothes, doing so more and more frequently. Looking back now, of course, I think that perhaps on a subconscious level I was making my own behaviour more and more extreme because I wanted to force the situation to a head. But even in my wildest fantasies – and God, I'd had a few –I would never have predicted the circumstances of my exposure.

The day it happened, I was working late. Charlotte had seen her last clients – a husband and wife who were celebrating his promotion by paying Charlotte to chain them together upside-down while she turned the hose on them – at 9 p.m. At 10 p.m. she said goodbye. I heard the front door close and Charlotte's expensive car purr away down the street. I set to work cleaning the wet room, working extra fast because I was in more of a hurry than usual to fool around and fantasise. I was trembling with excitement at the thought of tonight's session: the previous day, a new outfit that Charlotte had ordered from America had been delivered. Even she hadn't had a chance to wear it yet. I'd seen it hanging up in the wardrobe and knew that I had to put it on at the first available opportunity.

I held it up. It was a transparent plastic catsuit with matching Perspex-heeled shoes. The whole outfit left nothing to the imagination: its only concession to modesty a sprinkling of crystals around the nipples and groin area but they did more to draw attention to these erogenous zones than cover them up. Fingers fumbling in excitement, I took off my own clothes and then slipped into the garment, enjoying the way the tacky plastic tugged against my skin as I pulled it over my hips and yanked the straps over my shoulders. Oh, yeah. It fitted me perfectly: it was sticky but smooth on the inside: but the crystals that encrusted the outside were sharp and scratchy. Don't touch me, the suit seemed to say, or you'll get hurt, very hurt. I felt like Cinderella in a head-to-toe, deliciously kinky glass slipper.

The catsuit came with a bunch of accessories: there was a transparent plastic rope for tying up willing victims and a ball gag of the same see-through material but my favourite piece was a whip, its smooth glass handle attached to long, skinny plastic lashes also studded with crystals. I swished it this way and that, bewitched by the way the whip caught the light and refracted it into tiny rainbows on to my skin. All whips, I was beginning to realise, have their own voice. This one had a high-pitched swoosh which sounded beautiful as I brought it down on to the back-side of an imaginary slave. Just the sound of it was enough to get me wet between the legs. I felt my juices pool in the gusset of the catsuit and I thought to myself with a secret smile that I would definitely have to do a good job clearing up that one for Charlotte.

I parted my legs, held my arms aloft in a real don't-fuck-with-me stance and sneered at my reflection in the mirror. I closed my eyes and imagined what I would do if I had a slave here. I began to picture a faceless man prostrate at my feet, licking my boots, trembling under the force of my whip. I was just beginning to lose myself in the fantasy and feel the first familiar stirrings of orgasm when I heard the footsteps descend the steel staircase. My flesh turned to ice. I realised with a shock that in my haste to get down here and raid the dressing-up box I hadn't actually locked the door behind me. The footsteps could belong to anyone – a client, or, even worse, someone off the street. I was petrified in my pose.

'Hello? Charlotte?' came a voice I recognised. 'Mistress?

Are you there? I know I don't have an appointment, but I needed to see you. I've been bad, I've done some terrible things, and I really need a dose of your punishment.'

Howie. That American twang was unmistakable. As he got closer, I still didn't have a clue what I would do as he came in. For a few seconds we locked eyes and I saw him gulp in surprise. I thought quickly. I could do this in one of two ways. I could beg Howie not to tell Charlotte, plead with him to keep this secret and let me keep my job. But his voice had been trembling and his words highly charged. I wasn't sure Howie was in any fit state to reason with. Or – and the thought of this option made my plastic-clad pussy pulse a little faster – I could just go for it. I was in the right clothes. I was in the right frame of mind. I could really do this. I stamped my stilettoed heel on the ground so hard I thought the shoe would shatter and gave Howie the withering look I'd practised on all the imaginary slaves I'd fantasised about.

'Did I give you permission to speak to me?' I said, my voice pouring contempt on him.

'No,' he said, bowing his head.

'Look at the state of you,' I continued. 'You dare to enter my dungeon dressed? Where is your respect? Take your clothes off. QUICKLY!' Now it was Howie's turn to undress with trembling hands. He removed his expensive work clothes, hung them on the hook on the back of the door. The body that lay beneath was impressive: tall, broadly muscular without being too defined. His dick was thick and semi-erect between his legs, his balls shaven. I'll soon stiffen you up, I thought, as I squeezed my legs together.

'Tell me what you've done,' I said, pretending to inspect my nails. I kept my voice harsh and controlled, but inside I was going mad, my pussy pumping so hard I was sure it must be visible to Howie in my catsuit, the ultimate garment that gives a girl nowhere to hide. 'Tell me why you've been so bad, and I'll decide whether or not you deserve to be punished. Now, get down on your knees.'

He didn't obey me quickly enough, so I brought the whip down on the floor, inches away from his body. I noticed again how good his physique was: lean, gym-honed, he was obviously a strong, powerful man. All the more reason why having him in my thrall was the biggest kick I'd ever experienced in my life.

'On your KNEES, slave,' I snarled, enjoying the sight of this six foot six man prostate before me. Even in the flickering candlelight I could make out the scars from week-old lashes on his arse and thighs. As the whip came down, he closed his eyes and I heard him let out an involuntary whimper of pleasure.

'Confess,' I hissed like a snake, kicking him over so

that he lay on his back, utterly defenceless. I considered using the rope to tie him up, but instinctively I knew there would be no need. The power of my presence would be enough to bind him here until I chose to release him with a single word.

'I have bad thoughts,' he said. 'I want women to hurt me. There's a woman at work who treats me like shit and takes all my clients away. She lost me half a million pounds today, and as soon as I heard about it I had to go into the toilet and jerk off.'

'That's disgusting,' I sneered, even though I thought it was as horny as hell. 'You know what?' I continued, bending down until I was so close to Howie's head that I could smell the shampoo he uses and identify it. He shook his head. 'I'm sick of listening to your fucking shit. I'm gonna shut you up.'

And with that I put the ball gag on him. He looked so vulnerable there with the big marble stuffed in his mouth that I wanted to put my groin on his face and grind it into the gag, letting his muffled mouth bring me to orgasm, stifling his nostrils with the folds of my cunt. But I didn't, because I had power and control beyond any previous experience, and the wetness between my legs was growing by the second.

'I can't think of a punishment bad enough for a sad little prick like you,' I said, watching his dick come to life, my words caressing him to an erection as surely as any handjob would.

I picked up the crystal whip again. I wasn't going to use it on Howie's skin, but *he* didn't know that. The idea of being whipped, the thrill and fear of what I might do to him, would be hornier than the experience itself. I trailed the diamanté tips over his stomach, his inner thighs, gently flicked the underside of his dick and his balls. He was trying to shout something. I decided to take pity on him and whipped the ball gag out of his mouth. He took a couple of sharp breaths and then resumed his pleading.

'Oh fuck, I'm sorry, but I need to come, please let me come, oh God I need to come.'

'No,' I said. I had one more torture in mind before I was prepared to let him go.

Using the whip as a pointing stick, I trailed it along the shelf of dildos, vibrators and shafts that Charlotte uses on her clients. I knew where each one was: I cleaned and disinfected them all every night.

'Which one do you want?' I said, as if I didn't know exactly which one I have in mind. 'This one?' I held up a sleek chrome dildo a few inches thick. Howie nodded eagerly.

'Well, it's not up to you which one you get.' And I picked up a black rubber vibe that was twice as thick and twice as long as Howie's own dick. His eyes widened, in pleasure or fear I couldn't tell. It didn't matter – in the dungeon, pleasure and fear are one and the same. I poured a few inches of lube over the vibrator, ran my hand over the shaft, fought the temptation to turn it on, hold it against my clit and bring myself off.

Instead, I held the black rubber vibe in the crease between his twitching balls and his throbbing penis, using my hand to stimulate the length of his hard-on. When he was as hard as he could possibly get, I rammed it up Howie's arse, noticing as I did that his tight little hole was shaven. This made him seem even more vulnerable. This vulnerability got me even wetter. He was screaming for mercy. I varied the stimulation, knowing that I was pleasuring his secret hotspot, deep inside him, right behind his dick. He must have wanted to come so bad because he was almost in tears, but I would not allow him to submit to his bodily pleasures without my permission.

'Please,' he begged, in a pathetic little-boy voice that made my pussy swell even more, 'Please mistress, let me come.'

'Not till I say,' I shouted, stepping up the stimulation even further, wondering how long a man could possibly hold out. I waited until his body began to buckle and convulse, then bent down and whispered in his ear, 'You may release your juices NOW,' and gave the head of his dick a sharp tug. I could barely breathe as his soft, naked balls rose up into his body and his hot penis spilled forth a fountain of white milk that trickled all over my arm. I decided to give him one last punishment.

'Look at the fucking mess you've made,' I said. 'Lick that off.'

The sight of Howie's spent body in a heap on the floor, his head straining up and his white teeth and pink tongue slurping and sucking his own cum from the skin of my arm was more than I could take. I squeezed my thighs together, rocked forward and back a few times and experienced a silent orgasm that rippled through me like white heat. I glanced down at my body: my darkened nipples and flushed skin made it obvious I'd just come but I gave nothing away, waiting for a minute or two until Howie had licked every salty droplet off my skin.

'That's the end of that,' I said, partly because I wasn't sure what I did now.

'I don't think so,' said a familiar female voice behind me. I whirled around. Charlotte! The blood ran from my cheeks and I felt dizzy with shame and panic. Shame that I'd let myself get caught, panic that the best job I'd ever had was now over. Now that I'd climaxed, I didn't feel like a powerful dominatrix any more. I just felt like me, a cleaning lady with ideas above her station. And there was nowhere to go. I was acutely conscious of my nakedness beneath the thin, see-through garment.

But Charlotte wasn't angry. She was smiling. And, now that I looked down, so was Howie.

'I knew you had it in you the moment I saw you,' she said, looking approvingly at my body in the transparent catsuit. 'That's why I gave you the job. I guessed as soon as we spoke that you wouldn't be able to resist trying the whip on for size. And it suits you. You're a natural. Don't you think, Howie?'

Howie, still naked and lying curled up on the floor, nodded through his blissed-out haze. At that moment, I understood that it had been a trap – a set up to see how I would react when Howie turned up unexpectedly. I couldn't believe that Charlotte would be so devious, or that I had fallen for it.

'Are you going to sack me?' I asked.

'Oh, yes, I am going to have to let you go and get a new cleaner,' said Charlotte. I bit my lip, trying to hold the tears back. 'After all, you can't hold two jobs down at once, can you?'

'I don't understand,' I replied.

'Tina. You've seen how business is booming. I can't run this place all by myself any more. I need a new assistant. An eager, beautiful young dominatrix to whom I can teach the tricks of the trade and who can look after the clients I can't fit in. The job is yours if you want it. Do say yes.'

'Yes!' I said, tears of frustration turning to tears of pleasure and spilling down my cheeks. 'But there's just one thing. Who's going to clean this place tonight?'

'Howie!' barked Charlotte, suddenly in the mistress role again. 'You will spend the rest of the evening washing down this room as punishment for your disgusting thoughts.'

Howie looked at me and then at Charlotte.

'Yes, mistresses,' he said.

THE HITCHER

Think 'sex on the road' and you conjure images of steamy trysts with strangers at roadside cafés. That's the fantasy, anyway. But the reality is often the dull greyness of motorways and service stations and traffic jams. Alice and her boyfriend Paul had often shared their fantasies – but it wasn't until a chance encounter with a young hitch-hiker that they were able to turn their road trip into the ride of a lifetime.

Driving in the car is my favourite way to spend time with Paul. We work together, live together and play together so much of our lives is spent driving the country's roads in our vintage MG. I like to watch him as he drives, his lightly muscular forearm resting on the gearstick, his other hand on the steering wheel. Sometimes we find a local radio station and sing along with the tracks they play or listen to the local news. Other times, we'll stock the car up with our favourite CDs, create our own soundtrack.

But mostly, we just talk. We talk for hours. We reminisce about the good times we've already had, discuss our hopes and dreams for the future. And we also swap sexual fantasies. We play out imaginary scenes where we do depraved, delicious things to each other, describing our actions in explicit details. Some fantasy scenarios we really get off on but we only talk through once, like the story I made up about me being with another woman, or the one I told him where I tied him up and went down on him.

But there are some we return to time and time again and there's one in particular that has got us so hot that we've had to pull over and make love by the side of the road. It's the one where Paul describes how he'd like to see another man fuck me, how he'd like to stand there tugging at his own cock and balls while he watches me flat on my back with another man's dick sliding in and out of my pussy. And then I talk about feeling that dick while I watch Paul wank himself into a frenzy, watch one dick shoot a load of spunk into the air while another one pumps inside me. We've shared this fantasy so often that it's now my favourite.

We had no idea that one day it would come true.

We were driving back from a long weekend with friends in the West Country last summer. It had been a great few days that had been full of surfing and pubs and food and laughter. Our little car roared along the tiny uneven roads that wind round the English countryside like ribbons: we always prefer to take the back roads rather than the motor-ways. Paul was behind the wheel and I had my feet up on the dashboard, one arm draped over his shoulder. It was late afternoon, and the mood was calm and content, that Sunday feeling of tired but happy after a big weekend with good mates. Neither of us spoke, not wanting to shatter the holiday illusion, and certainly not wanting to think about going back to work tomorrow morning.

As we drove through Exmoor, dark clouds gathered above us and it wasn't long before the windscreen was covered in big, fat droplets of rain. One of those freakish summer downpours. The landscape was bleak and utterly featureless apart from one lone figure on the horizon.

'I wouldn't like to be out in this rain,' I said to Paul. As we drew nearer, we saw his outstretched thumb and realised he was a hitch-hiker: a young guy, no more than about twenty-five, dressed in jeans and a denim jacket, a rucksack on his back, and about to be drenched to the skin. He held out a piece of cardboard with marker pen scrawled on it but the rain had blurred the ink and his destination was illegible. Paul and I often saw hitch-hikers, and didn't usually stop for them. But this fresh-faced student type looked very different from the hippies we habitually whizzed past on the motorway. I glanced at Paul.

'Let's see where he's going,' he said. 'Give the poor

fucker a lift if he's heading east. We've hardly seen a car for miles and God knows who else he'll find to take him somewhere. I'd feel terrible if I left him standing by the roadside there, he'll get soaked.'

We pulled into the lay-by where he stood. Up close, he was younger than I'd previously thought. He was good-looking, though, light brown hair that curled to his shoulders and creamy skin stretched over sharp cheekbones. But he was wet, and getting wetter, and he looked absolutely wretched.

'Where are you going?' he said to us.

'London,' I replied. 'Where do you need to get to?'

'Er, yes. Great, me too.' He said. 'If you could give me a lift I'd be so grateful. I've been standing here for hours.'

'In you get, son,' said Paul. I giggled, nudged Paul in the ribs at his use of the word 'son'. Paul was only about ten years older than him, no way old enough to be his dad.

The lad opened the car door and slid across the back seat. 'I'm Jim,' he said.

'Alice and Paul,' I introduced the pair of us.

'Hi. And thanks again for the lift. It was just starting to piss it down. Hey, it's nice and warm in here,' he said, noticing our heated leather seats. 'I'm soaking. Do you mind if I just take my jacket off? It'll probably dry quicker off than on.'

'Go for it,' said Paul. I pulled the sunshade down and looked in the mirror so that I could see Jim in the back seat. He peeled off his light jacket to reveal a damp white T-shirt that clung to his flesh and I could make out tight pecs and a very fit body underneath it. My eyes skimmed over his form as he peeled off his T-shirt too and I was even more impressed. Slim but not skinny, toned and lightly tanned, Jim had that firm, defined flesh that comes not from dieting or working out in the gym but through youth. It was years since I'd been this close to a half-naked young man and it was wildly arousing.

The miles sped by and the three of us made small talk, my eyes on Jim in the rear-view mirror the whole time. We learned that Jim was a student, twenty years old – making him thirteen years younger than us – that he'd been down for a work placement interview, run out of money, and was trying to hitch his way back to his university in West London.

'Have you got a girlfriend, Jim?' I asked, innocently.

'No,' he replied, shyly.

'What? A good-looking young guy like you?' He blushed, which I found very endearing. 'But you must have had some action at university? A bit of experience? I know what you students are like. I remember when Paul and I were at college. Everyone was shagging everyone else.'

'Well, a bit, of course,' said Jim, defensively. 'But girls my age don't really do it for me. They're all skinny, miserable and obsessed with make-up and hair. I can't talk to them like I can to a woman a bit older, you know, like, your age. There's something sexy about an older woman, you know?'

'Calm down, Jim,' said Paul, in his teasing voice. 'Anyone would think you were flirting with my girlfriend.' Luckily, Jim had worked out that Paul was teasing him.

'Well, you know, who wouldn't?' replied the student. 'She's gorgeous.'

'She certainly is,' said Paul, sliding his hand over to my thigh and giving it a quick squeeze. There was an awkward silence for a few miles while Jim looked out of the window and I looked at Paul and I knew he was thinking what I was thinking.

'So what is it about Alice that you like, Jim?' continued Paul.

'Oh, leave it out,' said Jim, embarrassed again. 'I'm not trying to get off with her.'

'No, but if you were,' pressed Paul.

'Well, you did ask,' Jim replied. 'Okay. I like her shape. I can see she's got big tits, and I like that, it's womanly. I like her long curly hair and that she looks pretty and natural without make-up. And I like the fact that she isn't all done up like girls my age. Alice looks real and natural:

scruffy, but in a sexy way.' I looked at what I was wearing: a tatty old charity-shop sundress that I'd had for ever. But I did feel sexy in it: natural and fresh and free. I guess that was *my* brand of sexy. I noticed with pleasure that the rain had stopped and a lighter sky was on the horizon.

'You're a man of taste,' said Paul. 'Those are all the things I happen to love about Alice, too.' He paused for a beat. 'Well, that and the fact she's got the hottest, wettest, tightest little cunt I've ever had the pleasure to stick my dick into.'

'What?' gulped Jim, the way people always do when they've heard what you said perfectly well but they can't believe you actually said it. In my mirror I could see Jim blush but I also saw his hands were folded over his lap and I knew that Paul's words had triggered off the beginnings of fierce arousal. I thought of his young cock and balls swelling inside his jeans and I, too, began to experience a throbbing sensation between my legs.

'Alice's cunt,' said Paul, as matter-of-factly as if we were still talking about Jim's university course. 'It's fantastic. She's always wet and very willing. You should try it.'

I was so turned on by Paul's description of my pussy and Jim's reaction that my mouth had gone dry and I couldn't trust myself to speak. But now I forced the words out through my lips and turned around in my seat to look at Jim directly.

'Well, Jim?' I said, raising one eyebrow as he gulped and covered his lap. 'Would you like to fuck me?'

'Are you making fun of me?' Clearly he didn't believe we were for real.

'Oh no,' I said, reaching out a hand to touch Jim's thigh. 'It's a very genuine offer. You see, Paul has always wanted to watch another man penetrate me. It's just a little thing we talk about. And here you are, young, free and single, and you've said that you like the look of me, and hopefully Paul's description has sold me rather well. If we can find somewhere nice and quiet, Jim, would you like me to make your dick extremely hard so that you can stick it inside me?'

Jim nodded, a vein in his temple bulging. That got me wondering if his cock would be smooth or veiny, long or short. The subtle pumping in my pussy turned into a more intense pounding.

'Well,' I said. 'That's very good news.' And then, turning to Paul, 'Darling, do a left here. I think there's a place down here where we could all have a very good time.'

I directed Paul down a few more tiny lanes even further off the beaten track to where I remembered there was an old abandoned filling station. I would be the one getting filled today, I thought with a smile. We pulled into the deserted forecourt, shielded from the main road by overgrown brambles. As quickly as it had disappeared behind rainclouds, the sun came out again and began to bake the earth and the car was dry in seconds.

The three of us got out and stood facing each other on the forecourt, letting the sun warm our bodies for a while. We all knew what we were doing here but not one of us made the first move for what seemed like for ever, causing an atmosphere of increasing tension . . . and excitement. It took so long for anyone to do anything that I wondered if this is what they mean by an eternal triangle. I decided that if anyone was to get things moving, it should be me. After all, I would be the centre of the action, the focus of attention. Phrasing it in my head like that stoked my fire: it was really about to happen. This scenario that Paul and I had played through in our fantasy for so long was actually about to become a reality. I felt my legs weaken as my pussy grew warm and damp.

I took a step back towards the car and undid the top button of my dress. Jim, wearing only his jeans took a step towards me. I walked back again, undid two or three more buttons so that my flesh was exposed to the navel. Jim took two steps towards me, unfastened the rest of the buttons and slid my dress over my shoulders. He looked like he didn't know what to do with it for a moment, then hung it over a disused petrol pump.

So. I was standing in the open countryside almost

naked. I looked down at what I had on: a pink bra that was pretty and girly but the safety pin holding one of the straps together rather detracted from its sex appeal. Besides that I wore a pair of Paul's boxers and battered old base-ball boots. It was hardly a full-on burlesque outfit, but I had never felt hornier. And as I felt the stiffening in the groin that was now being pressed against my hips, I saw that my outfit was having a pretty strong effect on Jim, too.

'Wait there,' I said to Jim, not wanting him to get too horny, too soon. I knew that young men didn't always last the distance, and I wanted to ride his cock for a long time. I took another step back so that my calves were touching the bumper of our car. I kicked off one shoe, then the other, letting the old sneakers land a few feet away. Jim watched as enthralled as if I'd been sliding stilettos off while dancing around a pole. Removing my bra, I unfastened the catch, slipping the straps off my shoulders, leaving my breasts covered until the very last minute. I threw the bra behind me and heard a soft thud as it landed on the roof of the car. Jim watched my breasts, fascinated by them and that fat young dick bulged so hard in his jeans that it must have been agony for him not to touch himself.

I licked one finger, then another, pinched each of my nipples, rubbed the skin around them, took a nipple between each thumb and forefinger and pulled my tits out towards Jim as far as they would go before it started to hurt a little. That tiny bit of discomfort felt good, so I pulled them a little bit further. Then I let my right breast go: it slapped down against my ribcage to make a pendulous teardrop shape. Jim whimpered.

'Well, Jim,' I said and even I was surprised how breathy my voice was, 'I bet you haven't seen titties like these before. Do you like what you see?'

Jim nodded and I released my left breast so that it fell level with my right. Then I squeezed my arms together, pressing my tits close, enjoying how it felt to be so in control.

All I had on now was Paul's old boxer shorts. I knew that he wanted to play the voyeur, that he didn't want me to pay too much attention to him, but I had to include him for a while. I turned my head to the right to see Paul's dick straining against the material of his old beach shorts. He had that look on his face that he got when talking about this fantasy, only it was a million times more intense now that he was actually seeing it unfold before his eyes.

'You. Get your dick out,' I told him. 'I want to watch you touch yourself.'

Paul undid the buttons of his shorts and lowered them so that they stayed around his hips. That familiar prick of his was rock-hard and bigger than I'd seen it in years. His obvious arousal increased my own.

'Okay, Jim,' I said, turning my focus back to the student. 'You can step a little closer now.'

Jim leapt towards me so that his topless body was pressed against my nearly naked one. We didn't kiss; it was enough to feel the length of his flesh against mine. I felt my nipples harden as they rubbed against the warm, smooth skin of his torso. He was surprisingly hairless which made a thrilling contrast from Paul's hairy, masculine trunk. He wrapped his arms around me, trailed his fingers up and down my back, but I didn't want these soft caresses, I wanted to be ravished, devoured, fucked.

'Oh, Jim,' I said in that new voice I seemed to have borrowed from a porn star for the afternoon. 'Can't you help me out of these wet clothes?' And it was true, those boxers were absolutely dripping with my juices. Jim dropped to his knees obediently and used his nimble young fingers to peel the cotton away from my skin. Even my bush was damp with my own pussy liquor and he pressed his face between my legs and inhaled deeply. His nose touched the tip of my clitoris, which made me gush a little more. Not moving his face, he slowly eased the shorts down my legs and I lifted first one leg, then the other, and stepped elegantly out of my underwear.

From the corner of my eye, I saw a blur of flesh and I knew that it was Paul getting hard and horny. I didn't want to make eye contact because if I looked at him too often it would have burst the fantasy bubble where Paul is a voyeur, watching in secret. But I knew it was happening, knew he was watching, and that was turn on enough for me.

I spread my legs a little, letting Jim know that it was okay for him to delve deeper. I wondered if it was his first time probing a cunt with his tongue: reticent at first, he sniffed like a puppy tentatively encountering something new for the first time, trying to work out what it is and whether he likes it. But when his tongue tentatively flicked against my clitoris, he saw and felt my whole cunt spasm appreciatively under his touch. Once he'd seen what his tongue was doing to me, he got a taste for pussy and there was no stopping him after that. He darted all over my clit, he stiffened his tongue and gently inserted the tip into my pussy. My thighs were trembling on either side of his face. It was so intense I wondered if I might come there and then. While that would have been so easy, and delicious, I wanted to come around his dick, to have that solid rod of youthful flesh inside me when it happened.

'That's so good, Jim,' I told him, pulling him up by his hair. His face shone with my juices and he looked pleased, like a kid who's just been given a gold star by a teacher he has a crush on. 'But I'd like you inside me now.'

I let go of Jim's hair, turned around so that I was face-down on the bonnet and eagerly anticipated his fleshy spear. The fumbling of Jim's fingers on his belt buckle bought me some time to calm my pulse and make furtive eye contact with Paul. His dick quivered in his fist and he was stroking himself real slow, tugging at his balls. I know he always does this when he's trying to stop himself coming, trying to eke out the pleasure, and I was satisfied that he was enjoying this experience as much as I was. I felt the soft warm tip of Jim's prick poking around at my thighs, trying to locate my opening. He jabbed at my arse, which felt delicious, and any other day I'd have loved it but right then it was my hungry cunt that needed to be satisfied. I raised my hips a little, spread my legs as wide as they would go and when I heard him gasp I knew he'd seen the pink hole, ready and waiting for him. My tits were pressed down on to the car bonnet, pleasantly squashed beneath me when Jim finally penetrated me. It was bigger and fatter than I thought: the first cock, apart from Paul's, I'd had inside me for years. I could hear Jim's high, tight bollocks slapping on his thighs and mine as he pounded my pussy, screwing his dick all the way in, pulling it out, skewering me again, until I felt overwhelmed with the fullness of it.

Confident now, Jim pulled me back by my hips, ripped his dick out of me mercilessly so that it tugged my tender flesh, flipped me over and threw me back down on the car bonnet. We were face to face and I could see Jim's dick for the first time. His jeans were only down as far as his hips, and his cock was the crowning glory of an almost unbearably perfect body. Jim was like an ancient Greek ideal of male physical perfection: lean, long, athletic, with hips that tapered in at the tops of his thighs. His cock and balls were the same lightly tanned colour as the rest of his body, his full bush the only patch of hair – even what I saw of his legs were smooth and hairless. For some reason this made me feel incredibly turned on. I was enjoying the view too much to look at Paul, but I wondered what he was thinking as he saw the two of us. Was Paul horny for this fit young man, or for me, or the dynamite combination of both of us?

Jim's expression was deadly serious. His hands were on the inside of my thighs, forcing them as wide apart as they could go. I knew he could see a dripping slit and an eager, erect clit both competing for his attention. He bent down to play with my breasts, not suckling or gently cupping them as a man of greater experience would do, but frantically shaking them, mauling them, transfixed by the way they moved like jellies on a plate. It felt exhilarating, but I needed him inside me. I reached up to Jim, placed a hand on each of those snaky hips and pulled his pelvis towards mine, guiding his pulsing hard-on towards my sopping gash. He slid in easily this time, and penetration was twice as delicious and intense second time around, because this way he was at just the right angle for the bottom of his dick to massage my clit. He banged harder at first, but soon worked out from my moans and my reactions that the way to get me off – and to stop him coming too soon as well – was to exchange this pounding method for a slow twist and grind of the hipbones. These gentle undulations did more to propel me towards orgasm than anything else. I felt the pre-orgasmic convulsions rock my body and I relaxed. It was going to happen.

Seconds before I came, I turned my head towards Paul again. I wanted to heighten my climax by watching him. I saw his dick in one hand and his camera phone in the other, filming the action. He was not bothering to slow himself down any more, he was tugging his own prick fast and furious, and his whole body shook as he approached the point of no return. I breathed deeply, allowing the climax to wash over me, lifting me up, waves of pleasure enveloping my body. When I had my orgasm, I made a point of keeping my eyes wide open, looking straight into the camera as I wailed and moaned like a wild animal. Paul moved towards us, his spunk shot across the car bonnet and decorated my face, neck and tits.

At the sight of Paul's cum all over me, Jim couldn't hold back. Ripping his dick out of my hole, he took it in his hand gave himself one final squeeze, a jet of warm, white liquid landing on my belly and the bonnet. I rubbed the liquid into my skin, mixing Paul's spunk with Jim's, massaging myself as though it was an expensive body lotion.

The experience was so intense that we were all lost for words. We dressed and got back in the car and continued our journey, each of us lost in our own version of the experience we'd just had.

We drove in silence for a few miles. Jim fell asleep in the back of the car, looking far younger than his twenty-odd years. Paul and I whispered excitedly together.

'I can't believe we did it!' I said to him.

'You were so hot,' he whispered back. 'I can't wait to get back and watch that video I took. Of his dick in your hole. And my spunk all over your face. Christ, I'm getting hard again just thinking about it.'

'It's almost a shame he's still here,' I said under my voice, glancing back at the sleeping student. 'Funny, now that I've fucked him I kind of want to get rid of him.'

'Yeah,' Paul agreed. 'But what can we say? We used you, now please find your own way back to London? A promise is a promise.'

'You're right,' I reply, giggling. 'Although he might not mind. I mean, he's got a great story to tell his friends now, hasn't he?'

Somewhere in Hampshire, we got a little sleepy and decided that we needed a coffee to perk us up for the rest of the journey. We spotted another service station, fully operational this time, and pulled up to stretch our legs and refresh ourselves before the last leg back to London. As the car braked, Jim woke up.

'Oh, fuck,' he said sheepishly, embarrassed that he'd fallen asleep. 'Sorry. Are we in London yet?'

'Just stopping for a coffee,' said Paul. 'Do you want one?'

'I'll be okay with a can of coke,' Jim said. The three of us ambled over to the café. Paul and I ordered coffees while Jim bought a coke and drank it sitting outside. We took advantage of his absence to snuggle into a booth and replay as much of the video on Paul's phone as we dared. I felt a fresh seep of moisture between my legs as I watched myself remove my bra, teasing the poor young student.

'God,' said Paul, sensing my arousal, and slid his hand between my legs. 'I can't wait to get you home. I'm ready to go again.'

'Oh! *You're* like a lad of twenty, now!' We both started laughing.

When we finished our coffee and went back to the car, Jim was nowhere to be seen and his rucksack was missing from the back seat. Underneath the windscreen wiper was a note.

'Thank you for the best experience of my life,' it read.

'I will never forget it. Met some girls who are travelling to my campus and I'm going to hitch back with them. But I will be thinking of you.'

I folded the note into my pocket as a reminder and slid into the driver's seat. Paul climbed into the passenger side and we drove home.

THE DIAGNOSIS

I used to play doctors and nurses with my male friends and cousins when I was a little girl. Didn't we all? You show me yours, and I'll show you mine. I never imagined the grown-up version of this nursery game could be so much fun until Leila told me this story.

No real nurse ever dressed like this, with stockings and suspenders under a pelmet skirt that barely covers my modesty. As I squeeze myself into my fancy-dress outfit, I catch myself in the mirror. A nymphette nurse from a *Carry On* film pouts back. I'm not used to showing this much leg and I'm certainly not used to wearing stockings and suspenders. It's rather ridiculous and highly imprac-tical but I can see why so many people find it sexy. The tight, satin suspender belt is restrictive and the fact that my legs are encased in nylon net up to the thigh but that the air can caress my arse and inner thighs, my most private areas exposed, is really rather thrilling. I slip my feet into stupidly high, black patent shoes and smooth down my frilly white apron. I love fancy-dress parties, but I've never had an outfit quite this attention-grabbing and sexy before. My taxi-driver rings the doorbell and I climb into the cab, the sexy nurse speeding through the city streets on the way to what promises to be a fabulous party.

Lucy's party is in the penthouse bar of a huge entertainment complex on the river. I follow the banging music blaring out of the rooftop suite. Just to make sure I have the right venue, I also follow a gorilla and Charlie Chaplin up the stairs.

The party is buzzing and Lucy is dressed as Cleopatra. 'I'll have to introduce you to my colleague, Jay,' she says, and points across the room to a man in a white coat with a stethoscope slung around his neck. He can take my pulse any time, I think. He's gorgeous, with thick dark hair that falls just below his neck and straight black eyebrows, a strong nose and a full mouth.

'Good job you two are here,' says Lucy, looking around at all the very drunk people dancing in the middle of the floor. 'I've got a feeling there are going to be some casualties tonight.' But she doesn't introduce me; some more guests arrive and she's off, screeching hellos.

I'm too shy to introduce myself to Jay without Lucy as a go-between. It's daft, because our matching costumes mean I've got the perfect excuse to go and chat him up, but I just can't bring myself to. I down a glass of wine to give me courage and light a cigarette. Then I hear a voice over my shoulder.

'I'm afraid that as your doctor I must recommend that you stop smoking.' Without seeing his face, I know it's him. Jay. 'Not only is it very bad for your health, but it sets a terrible example when members of the medical profession smoke in public.'

I laugh, turn round and up close he's even hornier than he looked from the other side of the room. He's taller than me but not too tall, and his face is gorgeous, deep green eyes, pale olive skin but with high colouring in his cheeks and those lips, they're like two petals, more feminine than masculine, contrasting beautifully with the trace of stubble on his chin. Under that shapeless white coat I can make out broad shoulders and slender hips. I take in all this in a second.

'I do apologise,' I say. 'But I've had a terribly hard day on the ward, and this is the first chance I've had to relax. You doctors may be able to boss us nurses around in the hospital, but here you have no authority over me.'

He laughs too, and says, 'In that case I'll join you,' and whips a pack of ten out of his pocket. 'Hang on, I know I've got a lighter in here somewhere,' he says fumbling.

'Allow me,' I say, offering him my box of matches. When he leans in I can smell him for a split second and he smells good, sweet and creamy, the way some men do.

He pulls away to drag on his cigarette and all I can do is think about how I can get him to lean in close again.

'I'm Dr Jay,' he says. 'Thank you for the light.'

'Nurse Leila,' I reply. 'So,' I say, gesturing at a white plastic briefcase with a red cross on the front in his hand. 'What's in your bag?'

He smiles, flips it open. It's a children's toy medical case, with dummy plastic blood-pressure kits, a moulded plastic toy syringe and a reflex hammer made out of soft rubber. Looking closer at the stethoscope around his neck, I see that that's fake, too.

'I never travel without it,' he says. 'You never know when someone will need to be diagnosed with a mysterious illness.'

'Oh,' I say, returning his sexy smile. 'And do you think there's anything the matter with me, Dr Jay?'

'Well, Nurse Leila,' he replies. 'At first glance, you appear to be a specimen of rare physical perfection in rude health. Apart from your evil smoking habit, of course.' He sips his beer and takes a drag on a fag as he tells me this and I giggle, blushing, because he called me perfect.

'But of course to make any kind of real diagnosis, I'd need to do a more thorough hands-on examination of you. Will you allow me?'

'Of course,' I say.

'You must come into the light first,' says Jay, leading

me over to what is perhaps the darkest corner of the room, a little alcove with a picture window that looks out on to the river. He begins by breathing on his stethoscope. 'To warm it up,' he says. 'It can be very cold, and I'd hate to make you jump.' But it's not cold, it's warm to the touch as he slides it down between my breasts. His fingers close over it as he pushes it deep into my right breast, hooks it into his ears and pretends to concentrate. His fingers on my flesh are warming and arousing. The flesh of both my breasts begins to tingle and my lips buzz; I know that if this carries on, my pussy will start to throb and then I'll be in real trouble. I clear my throat.

'Excuse me,' I say. 'I think you'll find that the heart is on the left side of the body.'

'I know that,' he replies, quick as a flash. 'But how else do I get to feel both your tits?' And with that, he slides the palm of his hand across my breasts, so that he's now poking and prodding my other breast. He puts the heel of his hand down to where my nipple is, allows it to warm pleasantly. I feel my nipple harden under his touch.

'There appears to be some reaction in the left breast area,' he says. 'I'll have to make a note of that.' He unhooks his toy stethoscope from his ears, lets it fall away from my breast but his hand stays flat against my tit, my nipple getting harder all the time until it's so engorged that it's poking through my bra and pressing against the stiff nylon of my nurses' uniform. I look around the room. Can anyone else see me standing here like this, letting a complete stranger fondle my tits? And if they can, can they see the desire etched on my face? We're in the corner, and everyone's busy, but if anyone were to stand still and look, that's what they'd see. A doctor and nurse indulging in a very private conversation.

Jay takes his hand away. 'Right,' he says. 'Just a couple of extra symptoms to check you out for, and then I can make a diagnosis.' He brings out a tiny light, shines it in my eyes and leans in so closely that his breath plays upon my features. I could, if I wanted, lean in and go for the kiss now but despite what he's just done I don't know how to read him. All this baby-doctor-talk and flirty banter might be tongue-in-cheek but my desire is very real. My heart beats hard at him being so near and my body wants him to finish what he started when he placed his hand on my breast that time. 'Interesting,' he says.

Then he places a finger on my lower lip, forces my mouth open and says, 'Say aaah.'

I giggle as I try to make the noise he's after but I'm so distracted by the sensations all over my body that it comes out as a prolonged 'Oooooh,' more like a sigh I'd make during sex than one I'd usually let escape from my body during a routine doctor's examination. I bite down on Jay's finger, close my lips around it. I taste the salty sweat of his hands.

He leaves it there, closes his eyes, breathes deeply. I suck his finger like it's his cock, my tongue caressing first the underside of his digit, then the end, showing just what I can do with my mouth given half a chance. When he next speaks, he's the one with the wavering voice.

'I see dilated pupils and an increased heartbeat,' he says, half-joking, half-serious. Our bodies are almost touching and I can feel the heat from his radiate out towards mine. I wonder what it would be like to press ourselves together and my pussy pumps out a hot little rhythm in reply.

'I diagnose a serious case of sexual arousal,' he says. 'I'm afraid it's terminal. There's only one cure, and I'll have to administer it. But before I make sure, I need to do an internal examination.'

He bends forward so that the sides of his white coat hang like curtains obscuring my body from general view. We're looking each other in the eye, locked in this moment, silently daring each other to back down. The flirty banter of earlier has given way to something raw and powerful. I know that I'm about to cross a line. I want to.

Jay reaches between my thighs. My skirt is so short that access is unimpeded. His soft dry fingers toy with the suspender belt, tracing the skin on my inner thighs, sliding between the stocking and my flesh, before softly drawing my panties to one side to expose my pussy. I'm fluttering with anticipation and I can't believe I'm letting him finger me in the middle of this party. He runs his fingertips along my labia, probes the fold between my cunt and the tops of my thighs. I spasm, then relax as he inserts a finger into me. It's wet inside, and he swirls that finger around before drawing it out tantalisingly slowly and then pressing it gently against my clit. It's all happening so quickly; I can't believe I'm ready for it but I am. He rubs the eager little bud and my knees tremble beneath me. I stagger backwards leaning on the window for support.

Jay takes a step forward but doesn't break his rhythm of his fingers sliding in and out of my hole, round and around my clit. The cold glass soothes my aching flesh and I'm glad I've got something to lean on. The rushes travel along my limbs and my cunt swells and engorges, each tiny movement he makes getting me wetter and wetter and wetter. I close my eyes. If anyone is looking, I don't want to know, because I can't stop something that feels this good.

Jay takes his hand away from between my legs.

'Oh, you're definitely suffering from a severe case of nymphomania,' he says. 'It's the worst I've ever seen. There's only one way to cure it, I'm afraid,' and as he talks I see him tugging at his belt, loosening his trousers. 'An injection. Do you know what kind of injection?'

I nod. 'An injection of your big, hard cock,' I say and

at this I see a flicker of hungry desire travel across his features. I try to glance down, see whether his cock *is* big and hard, eager to set my eyes on it and get even hornier, but the shadow of Jay's white coat means I can't see anything. I pull the coat towards me, holding it out so that it makes a screen that no one will see through. To the casual observer it will look like we're deep in conversation. I hope.

'That's right,' he says, stepping in closer and for a few delicious seconds I feel the soft round tip of his prick prodding against my swollen clitoris. I'm so slippery that he glides into my slit with ease. I gasp with pleasure as his dick turns out to be both the biggest and hardest I've ever taken inside me. His legs are bent at the knee and he's thrusting into me, pulling out, pounding hard. He slides a finger between me and him, using his knuckle to make short sharp motions on my clitoris that precipitate the explosion.

I orgasm in under a minute, my cunt tugging and squeezing at his dick and he's a split second behind me. I come hard around his prick, milking it dry of spunk. We stay close, two pulses racing at a rate that any doctor would call terribly dangerous. Jay's hard-on subsides and I let the delicious aftershocks of my climax give his dick a few final squeezes. It takes longer to recover from the orgasms that it did for them to occur – from the moment of penetration to climax.

'So,' he whispers in my ear, 'Do you feel better now?'

'Oh, much, much better, doctor,' I reply, nipping his earlobe with my teeth. I look around the room over his shoulder. Everyone's too busy on the dance floor or indulging in flirtations of their own to pay attention to the two medical staff sequestered in the dark corner. I pull back my hips, ease myself gently off his dick and he tucks it back into his trousers.

'Glad to hear it,' he says. 'But I do hope that you have a relapse very soon indeed.' He puts a hand to my cheek, a hand that smells of my own cunt. And only then do we lean in for our first kiss.

WINDOW SHOPPING

～⚬～

*Sex in public is one of the most common fantasies there is.
And it's one of the hardest to fulfil, because carrying it out
involves taking a risk – a big risk. But Bethany, who told
me the following story, found out that the bigger the risk, the
greater the reward.*

I met Max at the designer furniture store where I work,
an exclusive little emporium at the expensive end of town.
I'd only been working there for a few weeks when he came
in to buy a new sofa. I noticed him as soon as he walked
into the store. He was sexy in an easy-going way with dark
brown hair that stood up in a messy quiff at the front of
his head. As soon as I saw his hair, I wanted to run my
hands through it, tug at it, brush it out of his eyes. I made
a point of going over and asking him if I could help him.

'Thank you . . . Bethany,' he said, reading from my
name tag. Later he told me he'd been pretending to look
at my badge but really he was trying to see down my top.

Max explained that he was kitting out his new bachelor pad. As I showed him our most cutting-edge, exclusive items of furniture, it became apparent that he had great taste and lots of money. He picked out a few cool pictures and an edgy, geometric sofa. When I was helping him to choose an armchair, he bounced on a leather chair and asked me if I'd like to sit on his lap. I would have liked to, very much, but it was neither the time or place.

'Not here, not while I'm working,' I said. 'But if you'd like to take me out to dinner, I'll sit wherever you like.'

Max picked me up from work three hours later when my shift ended, took me to dinner at an expensive restaurant and then on to a cocktail bar. I went home with him and sure enough I sat on his lap. Naked. For two hours. We've been inseparable ever since. I knew that night that I'd met my soulmate.

Like me, Max is what you'd call a classic show-off. He loves to watch us fuck, and we've filmed ourselves screwing from every angle, in every room of the house. When a shipment of huge designer mirrors came into the shop, I ordered one for him. It's floor-to-ceiling, and he loves to fuck in front of it, pounding my pussy from behind while we make eye contact in the mirror, watching each other's faces as we come. Sometimes he'd throw me against the mirror and fuck me right up against it, so that when we've finished, the sweaty outlines of our bodies are imprinted on the glass. And sometimes it is enough just to talk about what it would be like to have other people watch us fucking. How horny it would be to see them lose control as they watch his dick slide into me, as they watch our bodies tangled and struggling together. This fantasy never fails to get us both off. Like I said, Max is my soulmate.

When we'd been together a year, I thought that I should do something special to celebrate the fact that we were more in love and hornier for each other than ever. And by something special I didn't mean a new item of furniture! I wanted to give him a new sexual adventure, something he'd never forget, something that would gratify our exhibitionist streak. I thought about posting a film of us fucking on the Internet. I could just picture Max's cock getting hard as we broadcasted our climaxes for total strangers to watch. To know that other people out there were watching us, dicks in hands, vibes on clits? God, I got wet just thinking abut it. But I didn't dare to risk it.

I racked my brains for ideas, then one day as I put the finishing touches on a new window display, and people on the street outside stopped to watch me at work, it came to me in a flash. I knew just what kind of anniversary gift I was going to give Max.

When the day came, Max took me out to dinner to the very same French bistro he'd wined and dined me at the year before. Over the meal, we talked about our favourite subject: sex.

'I like your tits in that top,' he said. 'I can't wait to take you home and put them in my mouth.'

'I tell you what would be even hornier,' I replied, warming to the theme. 'If you did that here and now. If I just whipped them out, here in the restaurant. Look at that waiter – imagine how hard he'd get as he saw my nipples, how jealous he'd be. And that woman over there dining on her own. We could show her your dick, I could take it in my mouth, and she'd be rubbing her clit under the table.'

I kicked off my shoe and slid a stockinged foot up the inside of Max's thigh. I realised I was having the desired effect as my foot encountered a rock-hard erection. I pressed hard with the ball of my foot. He moaned, closed his eyes.

'Don't tease me,' he said. 'You don't know how much I'd love to fuck you in public tonight. But even I draw the line at nudity at the table. It's very bad etiquette.'

I giggled. 'Well, you'll just have to make do with whatever else I've got planned for you, won't you?' I said, raising one eyebrow.

'Plans?' said Max, looking excited. 'I didn't know there were plans.'

'Oh yes,' I said. But I won't tell you until after you've

had your coffee.' I've never seen a man down an espresso so quickly.

'Come on then,' he said. 'What is it?'

'Maybe I'll tell you on the walk home,' I said. 'But I think you'll like it.'

As we paid the bill and walked out of the restaurant, I had to laugh; Max was so hard that he couldn't stand up straight, and when the waiter tried to help him on with his jacket Max blustered saying that he'd rather carry it, thank you very much, and backed out of the restaurant with his jacket draped over his cock. It was less obvious to the casual observer, but I was pretty stoked, too – I was totally soaking at the thought of what we were going to do, apprehensive that I would actually carry it off, and wildly turned on by the hard-on that I could see straining against the fly of Max's trousers. When he did come he was going to shoot so much spunk into my hole that his balls would be completely drained.

Instead of turning right at the crossroads, I took a sharp left.

'Where are you taking me?' said Max.

'I've left something at work,' I said, trying not to let my voice betray my excitement. Max looked disappointed. Hanging around in my shop obviously wasn't his idea of a sexy surprise.

We got to the store and I stood outside the window,

looking at the bed on display, wondering if Max would figure out what I had planned. The window display I'd lovingly created looked even more impressive than it did by day: dramatic black-and-white bed in a deep-red room, kitsch and 1960s in style, lit by a few retro spotlights.

Max looked at me curiously.

'Want to go to bed?' I said.

'Oh you beauty,' said Max as the penny finally dropped. 'Let me at it.'

Using my keys, I let myself into the shop through the side door and punched in the numbers that disabled the main burglar alarm. We tiptoed through the shop towards the window display at the front.

'You clever, dirty little bitch,' said Max, slapping me on the arse. We stood for a while, hidden behind the head-board, looking into the street. It was deserted, and there was no guarantee that anyone would see us. It was possible that no one would come by at all. But they might – they *might*. And it was that possibility, that unknown factor that was the total thrilling thing. Who knew what an audience would do, how they would react? Would they be aroused? Watch open-mouthed? Or call the police? To Max and I, nothing was a greater aphrodisiac than risk.

We undressed behind the headboard, peeling off each other's clothes between stolen kisses and dirty words. When we were naked, we padded around to the window itself, stood in the spotlights for a few moments, taking in our surroundings. Max drew me towards him, picked me up, kissed me hard and aggressively and set me on the edge of the bed. I was wild with desire: so eager to begin that my whole body shook. Max gently pushed my shoulders back. I yielded to his hands and lay down. Max kissed and licked my foot, working his way up my ankles, calves, knees and inner thighs. When I could feel his breath on my pussy and I started to get really wet, he began all over again on the other foot. This time, when his head reached the hot, throbbing place between my legs, he rested his chin on the bed and blew gently on my clitoris. I began to feel the first gentle spasms that foreshadow an orgasm.

Max ran his hands along the smooth skin of my inner thighs. With one hand inside each, he pushed my legs apart as far as they would go. Then he pushed them a little bit further and I felt a build-up of a dull tension as the muscles resisted. I could feel his breath on my waiting pussy. He must have been able to see it twitching and quivering and desperate for his attention. He placed a kiss directly on my clitoris. He hooked his shoulders under my knees, so that my legs remained splayed, and used his fingers to part the skin around my clit, leaving it exposed to his warm breath. Then he went to work with his tongue, tracing tiny shapes around my clitoris, avoiding the bud itself. This let the orgasm build slower than I'd ever experienced before. Round, up, down, round, up, down, teasing me and keeping it steady until I cried out. Because Max had his back to the window, neither of us knew if we were being watched or not.

'Anyone could be looking behind us,' I said. 'Watching your arse, your beautiful toned arse, as you're down on your knees, eating my pussy, tonguing my clit.' His lips and tongue were busy, so Max didn't answer me with words, but he increased his speed and pleasure and slid his thumb inside my yearning hole and I knew that my words were turning him on.

'Oh, that feels good,' I said, and then I shouted, 'I feel amazing! I've never felt so fucking horny in my whole life!' Max slid another finger inside me and then another. He twisted his hand around, pushing my pussy to its limit. The circling of his tongue on my clit turned to sucking and as I felt the tiny nip of his teeth on that most sensitive part of the body, my body began to buck and my limbs thrashed wildly, rumpling the perfect monochrome sheets that I'd spent hours smoothing to perfection earlier. My orgasm took me over sooner that I'd wanted it to, and I hoped Max wouldn't think it was all over too quick. He maintained his rhythm for the few seconds it took for him to be sure I was coming. Then he pulled his fingers away and hardened his tongue, pushing it into my quivering pussy so that it had something to wrap around as the waves of pleasure died down. I kissed Max, tasting myself on him. I looked over my shoulder. There was no one there. No one had seen. I tried not to feel disappointed.

'Come on, Beth,' murmured Max, 'Your turn to give pleasure.'

My pussy lips were still tender and sensitive as I knelt before him and I winced as I sank to my knees. Max sat up facing the window so he'd know if anyone was watching: he promised to give me a running commentary if anyone should walk past.

'I want you to spread your legs so that people can see your arsehole and that swollen pink pussy,' he commanded. Thrilled by his explicit commands, I obediently splayed my knees, my still-swollen sex visible and vulnerable from behind.

I stared at Max's beautiful, hard dick. The skin was smooth and velvety. I put my lips together to kiss the tip, teasing him, swirling lips and tongue around it but not letting him enter me, daring him to penetrate my mouth without my permission. I could feel how excited he was; a drip of clear pre-cum fluid leaked from the tip and I relished its sharp saltiness. He lost control then, and pushed himself between my lips. I let my teeth drag ever so slightly against the lower underside of it, just to remind him that I was the one in control here. For a split second, I saw his face register this tiny pain that gave way to pleasure when I ran my tongue along the underside of his prick, massaging the most sensitive spot near the tip. With one violent thrust, Max was inside me up to his balls, filling up my mouth and fucking my face, deeper than I'd ever taken him before but still not deep enough. I wanted more of his dick deep in me, wanted to take it all the way down my throat. I embraced the gagging feeling, moved my whole head, determined to make him let go, to cry out. I felt his buttocks clench and knew he was at the point of no return. I gulped, wrapping my mouth round him as tightly as I could, and he threw his head back and he let rip with a slow, low growl. His warm white liquid burned the skin on the back of my throat, and I eagerly drank what I could, the excess spilling from my mouth on to Max's balls and legs.

A couple of cars went past but they didn't seem to notice us there. I knelt on the floor with my head in Max's lap, licking the spunk off his thighs. But the sight of those cars reminded us that we might still attract the audience we craved. After five minutes, I felt a familiar twitching in Max's dick, watched the spent balls swell again, saw the exhausted flesh come back to life. I put one of his balls in my mouth and sucked it, felt his prick stiffen against my cheek as he got hard again.

'Oh, baby,' I said. 'You're hard and horny. And I need

that fat cock inside me right now. I think we're ready for round two.'

I got on the bed on all fours, facing the window, arse in the air, nipples hanging down and tits swinging. I was thrilled to see that in the night light our bodies were reflected in the glass, the window acting like a two-way mirror so that we could make out our own reflections but see through those images on to the street in front of us. I tilted my hips up so that my arsehole and pussy were in Max's face, letting him know that I wanted to fuck in our favourite position, him pounding me doggy-style. It wasn't just so that we could see ourselves as he rode me: I'd had my clitoral orgasm. With Max pounding me from behind, I knew that I stood a good chance of experiencing a G-spot climax, too.

'Oh, yeah,' snarled Max, his cock easily sliding into my cunt that was still oozing and slippery from his tongue. Having him inside me so soon after my last orgasm made me ultra-sensitive; I could feel every inch of Max probing my slit, from the rounded tip that prised open my lips to the thick, veiny shaft that stretched my insides and filled me up. Once he was securely inside me, he reached around and fondled my tits, grabbing them like a wild animal, watching them slap against each other in the window-pane as my whole body was rocked by the force of his thrusts. I closed my eyes, all the better to enjoy the pounding sensation, and was just beginning to feel a tingling in my arms and legs when Max stopped dead. Absolutely still. I opened my eyes to see what the problem was, and that's when I saw them. On the other side of the glass. A young couple, about our own age, holding hands and staring at the shop window with an expression on their faces of purest shock. Or was it shock? Even as Max and I watched, their faces registered not horror, but intrigue and then desire. They exchanged a glance and drew closer, touching each other as they watched us.

'This is it, baby,' said Max, pulling his dick almost all the way out of me and preparing for one enormous thrust. 'Let's give them something to fucking well look at.' And he speared me so hard with his cock that I threw back my head and let out a roar of pleasure.

I let my eyes skim over the couple on the other side of the glass. The woman had absent-mindedly begun to fondle her breast: her jacket was open and I could see her nipples stiffening beneath her T-shirt. Without taking her eyes off me, she grabbed her lover's hand, pushed it to the crotch of her jeans. He pressed his dick into her back, reached around and started to rub her clitoris through the denim. He didn't even attempt to touch her skin but I knew from the expression on her face that he wouldn't need to. I knew what she was feeling: that state of arousal when you're so turned on, that the slightest stimulation can trip you over the edge into an intense, searing orgasm. I looked into her eyes, licked my lips and she mirrored my gesture, the two of us exchanging this experience, making each other hotter and hornier, neither of us daring to break eye contact. Without turning to look, she grabbed wildly at the man behind her, her hand making a pulsing little starfish as she reached desperately for his cock.

Glancing at Max's reflection in the mirror, I saw his face twisted with raw, animal lust. He looked so primal that just the sight of him made my cunt spasm around his hard cock and I watched his features contort with pleasure. I saw Max slide his thumb in his mouth. Knowing what that meant, I shivered with anticipation. Max flexed the lubricated thumb for me and everyone else to see and then deftly slid it into my arse, pushing my face and tits down into the bed so that they could see my back and my arse cheeks, making sure there was no room for mistaking just where his slippery digit was. This sent the couple on the other side of the glass to new heights of arousal: as they saw his thumb disappear between my butt cheeks. The bedcover muffled my screams as the pleasure became almost too intense for me to take.

The girl finally managed to tug the guy's dick free from his clothes. It bobbed bolt-upright between his legs, thick and fat. Her hands closed around the length of his hard-on and he tugged on his balls.

'Look at his cock,' whispered Max. 'Look how hard we made him get. Your tits. Your arse. Me fucking you. Me with my dick in your dripping cunt.' Max's words were like dynamite to me, but I was too far gone to answer him, overwhelmed by what I saw and felt. My body alternated between vivid sensations and numbness as Max's dick skimmed my G-spot over and over again.

The guy's hand was now down the front of his girlfriend's jeans. Maybe I was wrong about her: maybe she just wanted to feel his hand on her clit. I watched as his knuckles moved beneath her waistband. She was groping and grasping at her own tits, playing with her nipples under her T-shirt with one hand, the other hand tugging at his hard-on, massaging the length of it. Max and I were transfixed by the man's dick which seemed to grow bigger and bigger by the second. Through the window I could see the tip of his penis begin to twitch and moisten. I thought what a shame it was that I couldn't reach out and take his cock in my mouth, suck it dry of spunk.

The whole time, Max had his thumb in my arse as he was pumping my tingling pussy. A shiver began in my pelvis and flowed along my limbs, numbing my arms and legs: a dull heat spread out of my body as Max felt for my nipples and pulled my tits hard. I could take no more. It was time to submit to my orgasm. I yielded to the surge of contractions that sent pins and needles rushing all over my body. My pussy hugged Max's dick so tight that he reached his second climax in five minutes. I felt one, two, three sharp thrusts inside my still-spasming pussy and I heard Max exhale deeply, his hands letting go of my breasts as he grabbed hold of my hips to steady himself. I milked every drop of spunk out of that dick, and when it was finished, our juices mingled, spilling out of me, sticking to the front of Max's thighs, pale liquid running down my legs and arse.

As our orgasms subsided, the girl on the other side of the window came too, and hard: a damp patch appeared between her legs and spread, darkening the fabric, as her knees trembled beneath her. When the guy felt her juices gushing on to his hand, he came too, his spunk flying out of his dick in a perfect arc before hitting the window inches from my face.

I got off the bed, pretended to lick his jizz off the window from the inside, my naked body pressed up against the cool, cool glass. The woman moved towards me and licked it off for real, hungrily sucking up her boyfriend's spunk. I saw her tongue and lips moving as she slid her mouth across the glass, and I mirrored her movements, miming a kiss. When her hands touched the glass where my breasts were it was as thrilling as if she had placed her flesh against mine. She gave my nipple an imaginary flick, laughed, and then she and her lover, zipped up, linked arms and walked off into the night, glancing over their shoulders at the shop window before turning a corner and disappearing from our lives for ever.

Max and I enjoyed one last, intimate, tender kiss in the shop window and returned to the shop to dress.

'That was the best present anyone's ever given me,' he said, helping me back into my dress. 'I don't think I've ever come so hard in my life.'

'Me too,' I said, buttoning up his fly. As satisfying as the experience had been, my mind was still racing. I kept thinking about how horny it had been when the girl and I were both pressed up against the glass. The fact that she was an anonymous stranger was the big turn on, but part of me wished they had stuck around, that we had got to know them. We could have hooked up, all four of us. Something even more intense and amazing might have come of it. Before we left, I smoothed over the bedcovers and re-set the security alarm. No one would ever know we had been there.

I went into work the next day, and spent a restless morning daydreaming about what I'd done the night before. In the cold light of day, it didn't seem real, it seemed like an incredibly horny film I'd watched rather than an experience I'd actually had. But a faint white smudge on the outside of the shop window reminded me that my public fuck had been very real indeed. All day, I made excuses to look at the shop window, focusing on the tiny smear, remembering the man's dick as he'd shot his spunk at the window, and the girl's lips as she'd licked it off again. My pussy pumped and swelled every time I replayed the image of it in my mind. I couldn't wait to get home, eager to take Max to bed where we'd fuck again, retelling each other the horniest parts of last night's adventure and talking about what it would be like to fuck in front of another couple again, and maybe have them join us. I watched the clock, counting down the minutes before I could be with Max, touch him, talk to him.

At five to six, I prepared to shut the shop when two customers came in. Great, I thought, I'll never get home to Max at this rate. But as they came a bit closer, I recognised them. I saw a tall, good-looking man and a woman whose face had been pressed close to mine, on the other side of the glass.

EL RITMO DEL NOCHE

~

Helen always thought of herself as typically British: polite and reserved. If you were being unkind, you might even call her uptight. Casual sex was certainly not on her to-do list when she and her friend toured Southern Spain. But one balmy night at a fiesta in a tiny town near Granada, she found that even the prissiest English girl sometimes needs a little Latin in her.

It's 9 p.m. and the sun is only just beginning to set. A low red orb in a streaky amber sky hangs above the red and white roofs and walls of this small Spanish town. In the street beneath our balcony, the local youths climb trees without ladders, throw each other strings of lights, wind them around the branches and fix up banners between the buildings. All day people have been parading through the town, carrying statues and effigies, praying, marching and singing beautiful, ancient songs that I don't understand but are evocative all the same. But now the religious ceremony is over, the real festival is about to begin. I've been told that music fills these streets all night, alleyways will throng with bodies and that the dancing doesn't stop until the dawn breaks.

I step back from the balcony into our hotel room. The city is dressing for the evening: I should, too. Lara is massaging aftersun into her tanned, toned skin. As she smoothes the lotion into her limbs they become golden and glistening, and she reaches for a white sundress that shows off her tan to perfection. I look at the long, dark hair that cascades to her bottom. She's as brown and beautiful as any of the local girls, and I know that she'll be the centre of attention when we go out tonight.

I check my own reflection in the mirror: I am as pale as Lara is dark, skinny where she's curvy, nervous where she's confident, edgy where she's sensual. Lara has orgasmic sex with every partner she chooses; I have never come, never been able to relax that way, although I would never tell anyone this. I think I've been close a few times, felt butterflies in my stomach when I've kissed a boy, but those fireworks that Lara talks about? It's never happened to me. I guess some girls just aren't programmed to enjoy sex that way.

We've been travelling through Southern Spain for ten days now and while Lara fries herself in olive oil every day I've had to carry a parasol and smother my body in factor

50. I have nothing to show for my time in the sun but a smattering of freckles on my nose. Well, that's not quite true: my already blonde hair has been bleached almost white. Each fine, straight strand will look luminous tonight. I decide to wear the cobalt-blue sundress I've been saving for a special occasion. It makes my blue eyes, the only splash of colour on my milky-white face, stand out. I may not have many assets: but I know how to make the most of those I have.

Before we go to dance, Lara and I share a huge plate of paella in a restaurant in the town square, marvelling at the enthusiasm of the town's young people. Groups of beautiful young men stroll arm in arm through the square. Teenage couples kiss passionately, oblivious to the merriment surrounding them. Children, who, in Britain, would have gone to bed hours ago, sit on laps, crawl under tables or sleep on seats. Lara and I linger here, watching the people and absorbing the atmosphere. Even someone as English as me feels the tension melt away and I start to mellow. I feel my limbs loosen and I'm even breathing deeper, slower, more relaxed. We stay there until the square becomes so full of people that I don't believe there's room for a single extra soul, and a very modern soundsystem starts blaring out Euro house. Those not already standing leap to their feet and begin to dance where they are.

'It's early,' says our waiter as the clocks strike midnight

and grandmothers dance with toddlers to the sound of a throbbing disco beat. 'The night is . . . what is the word? . . . Still young!'

Lara and I walk through the streets together, happy just to absorb this wonderful atmosphere. We turn heads everywhere we go, all the boys looking at Lara in her white dress. She looks like a bride, a princess. I feel like a ghost by her side. Lara nudges me in the ribs.

'Helen!' she whispers, excitedly. 'You're a sensation!'

'Don't be ridiculous,' I say. 'They're all looking at you. They always do.'

'Don't be so sure,' replies Lara. 'Listen.'

And I do listen, and I hear that they're saying, '*Bianca Guapa*', which translated means 'White Beauty'. I become a pink beauty as I realise that they're talking about me.

'They've never seen anyone like you round here,' says Lara. You're a hit!'

Feeling a little more confident, I smile shyly at one boy in washed-out jeans and a pale-blue T-shirt. He's the only one not whistling or catcalling to me but I like the look of him the best. He looks like all the rest of them – tall, lean, tanned and chiselled – but he's silent, respectful and there's something intense about him that draws my eyes to his.

Lara gets chatting to one of the guys. Her Spanish isn't much better than his English, but even I know what *bailamos* means. It means let's dance. And so a group of us follow him down a side alley to a little flamenco bar that appears to be carved into a rough hole in the wall. Inside it's more like a cave than a club, the whitewashed walls curving over to touch each other in the middle, making a ceiling which hangs low over our heads. An old man plays guitar while the women dance and make animal-like noises, whooping and clapping and I know that I've stumbled across real flamenco and that the sexy, earthy beat has pulsed in this city for hundreds and hundreds of years.

All the local girls do the steps, managing to look sexy and elegant whether they're in high heels, trainers or flip-flops. This dance is in their blood, they were born to it. Lara doesn't have flamenco in her blood, but she embraces the spirit of the dance nevertheless, letting one of the local boys whirl her around by her hands until her hair flies out behind her and her feet are a blur. Even I can tell that she's absolutely hopeless, but she's trying, and she's enjoying herself, and that's what people find so attractive about Lara. I order myself a glass of sangria, content to watch her make a fool of herself, happy to blend into the background here in this club where the walls are the same colour as my skin and my hair. But the boys have other ideas. They grab me by the hand, refusing to take no for an answer. I giggle as a couple of them whip me around, my feet all over the place. It's fun. Lara looks at me with pride in her eyes: I can tell she's pleased that I've begun to relax and show a bit of spontaneity for a change. Well, there's a first time for everything, even if I do spend more time whipping my feet, in open-toed sandals, away from the stomping shoes of the locals than dancing. I'm passed from boy to boy and the whole experience is a blur of denim and strong brown arms and curly hair and white smiling teeth.

And then suddenly, I am still, and I'm in a different pair of arms. Whereas other hands had grabbed at my body, these arms pull me softly towards someone new. I follow as if in a trance, this boy in the baby-blue T-shirt, to a corner of the bar. My heart is beating fast as I dance with him. There is a chemistry between his flesh and mine that means I am transformed from a gauche, awkward girl into a real dancer. I am suddenly able to feel the music. My feet move in time with his and my body is fluid and responsive. I have never been much of a dancer except at student discos and at friends' weddings, but here, in a cave in a small town, with a stranger and with only the most basic music, I feel my body open up and I let the sound flow through me and tell my body what to do.

'This is amazing!' I say to him, breathlessly smiling up at his big brown eyes. 'What's your secret? Who taught you to dance like this? Come to think of it, what's your name?'

He doesn't reply but smiles shyly back and that's when I realise that his English is almost non-existent. He speaks three words in a soft voice that makes me shiver from head to toe.

'*Guapa*,' he says, stroking me, his tanned hand tracing the skin just above my cleavage and making my breasts tingle with desire. 'Snow White.' He must have learned that from the Disney film. I look at him and realise he's very young – he can't be more than nineteen or twenty. I press against him, trying to know his body and encounter the slim hips that only young men on the threshold of adulthood have. I let my hands wander down to firm, skinny buttocks and sink my face into a hard, warm shoulder. And all the while we're dancing, but it's something that might stop being dancing if we let this go on much longer, because I feel the kind of sexual arousal that I've only ever known after about six dates and twenty minutes of foreplay. Here with this boy, this stranger, I am shrugging off ideas I've held all my life about what's wrong and what's right because my body is taking over. I'm slowly realising that there are a lot of amazing things I might be capable of tonight, and that dancing is just one of them.

That's when the doors to the bar burst open and another band of people throng inside, waving banners, carrying castanets and guitars, singing and packing the dance floor tighter than ever. Before I have a chance to object, a guy pulls me into the middle of the room where I carry on moving to the music, allowing myself again to be shoved from one partner to the next. But I never lose eye contact with my favourite dancer, always making sure that I know where he is, not wanting to break the spell, knowing that I'd come back for him, later. But then there's another crowd surge and the dance spills out into the street, I can't believe a little alleyway this tiny can contain so many heaving bodies. But it can and it does. I'm getting further and further away and then I've lost him, his wavy brown hair just another head in this surging crowd.

Then I see a face I do recognise. Lara, flushed cheeks beneath her tan, one of her shoes in her hand, a broad grin plastered across her face.

'Helen,' she shouts, grabbing me by the hand and pulling me towards the edge of the crowd. 'I've made a new friend! Come and meet Paco.' She gestures towards a burly young Spaniard in a grubby T-shirt. 'I know, he doesn't look like much,' she says sotto voce, 'But you should see the way he moves. There's something about a boy who can dance, don't you think?'

'Oh yes,' I say, more to myself than to Lara.

Paco leads us back through more crowds. Street lighting is poor and intermittent, so we have to rely on the odd light from a bar or club spilling into the street, illuminating just a few feet. It's hard for me to make out the features of the faces that pass by me in this half-light, and despite the size of the crowd, none of the men I pass are him – the only one I want. I pray for him to find me, I will it to happen. I feel that if he is near me I will know, that our bodies will draw together like two magnets. Now that he has begun to awaken something in me, every body that I pass on these streets makes my flesh tingle when they touch me, but none have the power to set my skin alight, not like he does.

We end up in the main town square which has been turned into an al fresco disco for the evening. Dance music blares out and some very dirty dancing is going on: the lambada and the tango are performed to chart hits. I watch the couples as they all move together in perfect time, reading each other's bodies and knowing when to turn, when to step forward or back, when to lead and when to let their partners take over. I'm jealous because I want to move with someone like that. I look around to see if he's there but somehow I know that this public, brash, dirty dancing isn't his style. My intuition is that he is sensitive and private.

There's nothing sensitive and private about Lara and Paco as they move together, taking centre stage and dancing on a stone plinth in the middle of the square. From my position leaning against an olive tree I'm half-aroused, half-embarrassed to watch their gyrations that cross the line between dancing and foreplay. She slides her hands up underneath that greasy T-shirt of his, revealing a surprisingly firm belly underneath, while his hands are on her breasts and then he's playfully slapping her arse. I feel another stab of jealousy. Lara has boys after her like this all the time, I never get to meet anyone who turns me on and now that I have, I've lost him in a crowd. I envy Lara's casual sexuality and her confidence. When Paco slides a hand between Lara's thighs and she tilts her pretty head back with a sigh of ecstasy I feel jealous and also a little aroused. I watch them, imagining that it's my pussy being felt through my panties, that it's my body pressed up close to a man who makes me feel alive, horny, feral.

When Lara drags Paco over to me and asks me if I mind if they go back to his place for an hour or so, I'm not surprised. I don't begrudge her, either. I'm happy for her, and besides, it's 5 a.m. and I'm tired. The walk back to our hotel is short and well-lit and I don't mind walking at all. The music still booms as I take a left into the cobbled narrow alleyway that leads to our accommodation.

I step over empty wine bottles and bend down to pet a stray cat who shoots out of a hidden door in a wall to see if I'm carrying any food. I have no food to offer, but the cat is beautiful. I'm stroking her soft grey fur when I feel something like a magnetic pull in my body, an awareness of the heat of another person. I hardly dare to look up, but when I do he is there, standing in the doorway, legs crossed, arms leaning on either side of the doorway, shirt riding up to reveal a lean stomach, a pair of snake-hips protruding over the top of his low-slung jeans. And a soft, gentle face that's smiling. When he extends his hand, I don't hesitate to take it. He pulls me through and gently closes the door behind him.

I find myself in a tiny courtyard garden. We can still hear the music from the square and he pulls me to him and we dance, moving together as though we had never been parted. In my heels, I'm almost as tall as him. Our hips are perfectly level, and his bony pelvis grinds into my own slender body and I feel the growing bulge of his dick as it swells and hardens between his legs. But he doesn't force himself on me; he lets the gentle undulations of his body teach mine how to move and slowly, slowly, that fire that I felt before is kindled again. Gently, he places his hands on my buttocks, using them to guide me, and my body turns to liquid I sway with him. He puts his hands on mine and raises them over my head: we remain joined at the pelvis, swaying together, our bodies communicating in a way that no words ever could. I feel the lean flesh of his chest press into my small breasts and they began to stiffen and harden. Slowly but surely the heat rises in my body and my pussy starts to skip and flutter.

His kiss is a natural progression. It starts soft and dry. Slowly, he slips his tongue between my lips. He begins exploring my mouth and gently nibbling, probing, wanting to know me. I feel a surge of desire, a gentle fluttering between my legs and a seeping of wetness. He kisses me again, the soft stubble of his chin scuffing my lips. He tastes of red wine and seafood and olive oil. I kiss him back urgently, growing more confident and passionate by the second. In response, his hands travel up my thighs, smooth and nimble fingers unhook my panties and slide them down my legs in a fluid, sexy motion. All the time we are both of us still in rhythm with the music. His hands are on my breasts now, pulling my dress down so that my nipples are exposed. My pale skin shines in the moonlight but my pink nipples harden and darken as he strokes my breasts, my neck, my shoulders. I unbutton his shirt with trembling hands, desperate to feel his skin against mine. When my breasts press against his chest, the heat from his body warms me and shoots bolts of pleasure running through my veins. Still we sway together in time to the music, in no rush, content to enjoy the sensation of my budding breasts rubbing against his skin, the light dusting of hair on his chest creating a delicious friction between our two bodies.

Then his hand is flat and motionless against my pussy. His palm gently undulates, subtly stimulating my pudenda, causing a warm trickle of liquid to ooze out of my pussy and pool in his hand. Inserting a fingertip between my yearning pussy lips he spreads my natural lubricant all over my clitoris, fondling and stroking with a movement as smooth as his dancing. I'm pumping hard now, my clit and pussy throbbing, a beat so loud and insistent I'm surprised it doesn't drown out the music and the crowds.

I free his buckle and thread his Spanish leather belt through the loops of his jeans, unbutton his fly, release the cock that is straining against the washed-out denim. I see it in the pale light: beautiful, young, hard, mine. It is smooth, the same olive brown as the rest of him, and trembling with anticipation, a fat tear of pre-cum oozing from its tip.

He continues using the juices from my pussy to smoothly circle my clit until he's sure I'm ready. When he slips a thumb into my convulsing cunt, I nod, answering his unspoken question. He drives his cock into me tantalisingly slowly, filling me up again, and again, and again, pulling out to penetrate me anew. I dig my fingers into his arse, driving him deeper and deeper and deeper, feeling the length of him inside me. The base of his dick is right where I need it to be, rubbing away at my clitoris. I can feel something delicious bubbling up inside me. It's a new feeling, and I know I'm about to experience my first orgasm. All the while, he's kissing me softly, and everything he does he does slowly. I close my eyes, dizzy with pleasure, letting my body dance and be led by his. I feel him tense and know that he's coming, and as the base of his dick grinds hard into my clit, a rush of pleasure comes from nowhere and turns my body into a series of warm, wet peaks of pleasure. My orgasm is an eruption that makes me cry out in joy and sweet relief. I have never known such intense bliss. I had no idea that I was capable of feeling something so beautiful. A tear of joy splashes down my cheek and on to my exposed breast. My dancing partner kisses the salty droplet on my nipple, slides his lips and tongue upwards, chasing the track of my tear, planting a dry, tender kiss on my cheekbone and then another on my smiling lips. We move together and dance while he's still inside me, letting his spunk trickle down my legs, his dick contracting, our mouths lazily exploring each other.

The first pink light of dawn pierces the sky and the courtyard is bathed in a rosy glow. At the same time, the music from the square comes to an abrupt end. The disappointed roar of the crowd confirms that the party is over. My dancing partner peels his body away from mine and uses my panties to mop up the liquid that trickles down my inner thighs. With a wink, he rolls up the sopping cotton bundle and puts it in his pocket. I kiss him one more time and then I'm gone, through the gate, staggering the thirty metres back to my hotel. In my bed, I lie awake for an hour, thrilled, grateful, happy, until finally I drift off to sleep.

Lara's hour of passion with Paco must have gone on longer than she expected, because it's 9 a.m. when she bursts into the room, waking me up, babbling excitedly about Paco's prowess between the sheets. She jumps in the shower and is still talking as she dries herself and clambers into bed.

'Oh Helen, I wish you'd met someone,' she said. 'You could have so much fun if you just loosen up a bit.'

I say nothing. What happened to me is not for sharing: not with Lara, not with anyone. It's a perfect memory of two people who came together one hot, steamy night. I roll over, close my eyes, feel my body thrum and throb in memory of the rhythm of the night.

GOING, GOING, GONE

Some of the most beautiful, confident, powerful women I know are also the ones who get off on surrendering to another person's will, to allow their bodies to become someone else's plaything for the night. Abigail is no exception. She's a smart, sexy woman. Strong. In control. I wasn't surprised when she told me she likes to be dominated. She's tough. She can take it. She needs it. You see, by night, Abigail likes to sell her body to the highest bidder and submit to whatever pleasures – and pains – that bidder will offer her.

It's night-time and I'm driving across London alone. It's so cold outside that I can see people's breath turn to mist on the streets outside. Everyone is dressed for the cold, in faux fur and leather, hats and scarves and gloves. If anyone looks in my car, all they'll see is a woman dressed in a very respectable trench coat, her red hair in a chic bob, nothing out of the ordinary. What would they think if they knew what lay beneath the coat? I laugh at the very idea and buzz with excitement in the knowledge of my sexy secret.

Because tonight I'm going to do something amazing, something I've never done before, something that has me wet at the very thought of it. Beneath my conservative coat, my body is bound in lace and leather. But no one outside my car knows this as I drive through the streets of the West End and through to the City. I wind my car through the old, narrow roads. This place where I earn my living in a skyscraper during the day is deserted on weekend nights. I've got the streets to myself and I turn the car stereo up loud, psyching myself up for what's in store. As though I need the extra excitement. As though I'm not already surging with adrenaline. I turn into a tiny cobbled alley. To the uninitiated it doesn't look like much: a few garages and old buildings. But to those in the know, this place is the centre of the universe – for one night a month at least. I fumble in the glove compartment for the laminated permit and show it to the black-clad guy who stands outside a large steel door. He looks at the pass, then at me. He gives a nod and then the door opens. I steer my car down a steep ramp and into the underground car park.

I look around: the car park is nearly full although I'm the only person down here. I look around at the other cars: they're expensive, nothing flashy or outrageous . . . nothing to indicate that their drivers are wild, experimental, sexy people. We all share the same secret. I take off my trench, fold it on the passenger seat. The cold air hits my skin like a delicious slap, and I check my outfit to make sure everything's in place. The ripped fishnet stockings which cover my legs are there, disappearing beneath a short leather skirt and the peephole leather bra is in place. In the cold air, I watch my nipples, forced through the tiny holes, become harder. I kick off the comfortable flat shoes that I use for driving and pull on the final part of my costume, a pair of boots with thirteen buckles and five-inch heels. What would my straight-laced colleagues, let alone my employees think, if they knew that I swapped my skirt suits and court shoes for these extreme items at the weekend? As always, it takes a few moments for me to be able to balance in my skyscraper boots. My whole posture alters, my tits are pushed forward, my arse tipped out, and every curve of my body is exaggerated. Walking in these things is torture, I think to myself as I take my first faltering steps of the evening, staggering like a baby giraffe finding its feet for the first time. When I'm sure I'm steady on my feet. I whisper out loud the word 'torture' and thrill at the way my pussy reacts to it. I find the sound of that word as thrilling as any caress or slap: it's foreplay I can do all by myself. Smoothing down my hair, I check my reflection in a metallic car door before making my way to the private lift that will take me one floor up and into another world.

The lift doors open on to a girl with a clipboard who lets me through with a smile when I show her my pass. I haven't seen her before; she's cute, with dirty-blonde hair and a chipped front tooth that I find deeply sexy. And so I walk, head held high, nipples arriving before I do, through to the oak-panelled, velvet-curtained room that has been transformed into a garden of pleasure and pain, just for one night, just for us.

I know a few people from the scene and we chat as I sip my orange juice. I get a few compliments on my outfit and when I tell old friends what I'm doing here tonight, they raise their eyebrows and rub their hands together in anticipation. I wander around, watch a stunningly beautiful young man yelp and yowl with pleasure as a dominatrix who's twice his age and half his size inserts a buttplug with a ponytail on it up his arse and twists it, stimulating him until he begs for mercy. In another dark corner, a gloriously, unashamedly fat woman sits on another girl's face while a man fucks her in the pussy. I feel free, blessed to have access to this place where anything goes. The motto here is that if another adult consents to it, you can do it: and my eyes take in dozens of adults who are not only consenting but begging for sex, for attention, for torture. I'd love to reach out and touch some of these players, to join in the games, but tonight I must restrain myself. I look at my watch, the hands just visible in the flickering half-light. It's 11.30 – half an hour until the main event begins. The event which I am part of . . . which I may even be the *star* of.

At the stroke of midnight, the clanging chimes of a grandfather clock sound and the club falls silent. We all know what this means: at midnight, the slave auction begins. Various men and women are offering themselves as slaves for the next four hours to the highest bidder, agreeing to hand over their bodies to the whims of another. The bidder can be male or female, and the winner gets to use and abuse their slave until one – or both – parties end up begging for mercy. And I have put myself up for auction. We're raising money for a local sex-workers' charity and although it's great that someone benefits, my primary motivation is self-gratification. To be at a stranger's mercy all night, to relinquish all power and hand over my body for pleasure and pain – oh God, I'd pay good money for that. I'd give up all my money for that.

The girl with the clipboard ushers me to the side of the stage. I'm always nervous before I relinquish control of my body, even though I know the results will be orgasmic. It's not fear so much as a rush of adrenaline and anticipation and an impatience to cut through the formal-ities and get down to it, start fucking, now. The club's MC, who will act as auctioneer for the evening, takes to the podium in the centre of the stage. His name is Leroy, and I've known him for a few years. He's beautiful, a mixed-race dancer with shorn brown hair and shining skin. I've had a crush on him since I first set eyes on him, but I'm pretty sure he's gay. Tonight he's showing off his ripped dancer's body in a pair of skin-tight lederhosen, which outline his generous cock and balls, and industrial, workman-type boots. As I take my place on the stage, I give him a playful slap on the arse and whisper that it's a shame he's doing the auction, that he's not out there as a buyer. I'd love to have some time alone with Leroy, especially as I hear he's a really evil master, to have his brown body bend my white one to his will. But as I scan the crowd who have gathered in front of the platform, I realise that tonight the place is packed full of sexy, glamorous people, many of whom, like me, work in the City and earn six-figure salaries. There's gonna be a lot of money raised tonight. And the successful bidders will want value for that money. The play tonight is going to be extreme. I resist the temptation to fondle my rock-hard nipples through my peephole bra.

To distract myself, I look around at the other slaves waiting by the side of the stage and we all smile our hellos to each other. There are three women including me and three guys up for auction tonight. While Leroy announces the auction, explaining the rules and talking about the charity angle, the clipboard girl chains us all together with heavy iron manacles at the ankle and wrist. They weigh my arms down by my sides and the heavy metal bites into the flesh of my leg, my first taste of pain of the evening. Just the knowledge that it's too late to back out now is thrilling. The six of us are led up on to the stage to cheers and whoops. I am last in the chain. I exchange a glance with my fellow slaves; like me, they're all glassy-eyed, breathing hard, hoping that a strict, disciplined master chooses them, nervous yet exhilarated at the same time.

Leroy casts an admiring glance at us before beginning his auctioneer patter. He starts at the opposite end of the chain. It looks like I'll be up last. That's fine by me. I love standing here, pussy throbbing, tits on display for all to see. The longer I stand here, the more excited I'll be when I'm finally released. And it gives whoever buys me time to think up lots of sophisticated, exciting things to do with me.

'Lot one is Andre,' says Leroy, describing a well-built guy in his late thirties. 'A real bear of a man, but he loves nothing more than being dominated by a skinny guy.'

He doesn't get any further into his pitch when two guys start a bidding war. One of the guys bidding has one hand on his dick and the other in the air, forcing the price higher and higher. The other one, not to be outdone, is holding a up a riding crop, tilting the tip of it ever so slightly whenever he wants to indicate a higher bid. After a few minutes, the two men talk to each other in low, urgent voices. Riding-crop guy takes to the stage and whispers something in Leroy's ear. Leroy nods and then announces that the two guys are going to pool their resources and share Andre for the evening. At the knowledge that he's going to have two cruel masters, not just one, Andre's face breaks into a smile and his dick begins to bulge beneath his leather pants. They raise £6000 for the charity and everyone's cheers raise the roof of this little club. Clipboard girl releases Andre from his shackles, and this big, burly man immediately bows his head in meek submission. He avoids eye contact with his masters as one of them puts a dog collar around his neck and leads him to a dark corner. The last thing I see is Andre's generous flesh wobbling as a riding crop is brought down sharply on to his buttocks. The sound of leather slapping skin, and Andre's deep growl of pleasure is too much for some people to resist, and a few members of the crowd who don't want to miss out wander away from the auction to look. For the first time I begin to panic. What if I'm left up here and everyone has gone away to watch the successful slaves. And another, more terrible thought: what if no one wants me? I am so psyched up for being someone's slave tonight. If it doesn't happen, what will I do with all this wild sexual energy that's pulsing through my body, making me feel more alive than I ever have done before, turning my pussy into a hot, pulsing wetness that craves stimulation? What will I do if it doesn't happen?

Actually, I needn't have worried. The rest of the auction passes in a blur, as one by one all the slaves are snapped up. I'm disappointed when a tall, blond guy I liked the look of picks another girl, because I wouldn't have minded him being my master. There was a Germanic hardness to him, mercilessness behind his cold blue eyes, that I wanted to experience. The other girl squeals with delight when a curvy young woman in a red catsuit slashed at the crotch pays £4,000 to buy her. I'm not disappointed by this. I like to be dominated by women, some of the best sex I've ever had has been with powerful mistresses who knew just how to bite a nipple and torture a clit, but tonight I want to play with a man. I want to feel overpowered by the size and bulk of a fit male body. I want his hairy roughness to contrast with the smooth vulnerability of my own skin. And most of all, tonight I'm in the mood for cock, a rock-hard fat cock that fucks me ruthlessly. While I'm losing myself in the fantasy of the perfect master with his perfect dick, rich-looking, glamorous women in their forties spend more thousands on the remaining two guys.

And then it's my turn. I quiver with excitement and spread my legs, showing any potential buyers what an eager little slut I am, sticking my nipples out. The more

I tease and tantalise the audience, the more wanton my behaviour now, the crueller my punishment will be.

'Our final lot, an exquisite white slave,' announces Leroy, pacing the stage as he assesses my selling points. 'Tight little tits that are already bound, shoes that mean she can't run away . . . this one's going to be a great little plaything for someone. And look at her,' he continues, flicking an exposed nipple and watching my cheeks flush a deep red with pleasure. 'She's ready for it. She can take whatever you throw at her. She wants it.' The sound of his rich, mellifluous voice combined with the electric shock of his finger on my nipple brings me sharply back into the moment. The first drop of juice escapes from between my pussy lips. 'So,' asks Leroy. 'Who's going to give me £100 to take this horny little bitch off my hands?'

The bids begin at £100 and immediately climb to £1000, then £2000. Because of the spotlight which is trained on me and shines right into my eyes – and is deliciously warm on my trembling tits – I can't see every person who's bidding. I quite like the look of a silver-haired man in the front row. He looks like he might be the kind of person I trade with at the bank, and people with that kind of money are always the most deviant fuckers out there. I should know, I'm one of them. A pretty, mild-looking girl who can't be more than about twenty shakes her head sadly when my price tag rises above £3000. Despite my desire for cock, I'd quite liked the look of her. The quiet ones are always the strictest mistresses. I love being objectified like this, I love the fact that I am property. I, who hire and fire and have all the power and money I want in my working day, am suddenly helpless. Leroy is also taking bids from someone else – male or female, young or old, but I can't see them in the shadows at the back of the club. I part my legs further, my micro-mini skirt showing just a hint of glistening pussy, and my price tag doubles to £6500, the highest price of the evening so far.

'Am I bid £7000?' says Leroy to the mystery bidder lurking in the audience. 'Lot six, going for £7000. At £7000, lot six. Going, going, gone.' He bangs his gavel down on the podium and it sounds like the crack of a whip. I stare as hard as I can into the blackness, straining my eyes until they water, eager to meet my master or mistress, but no one is forthcoming. I look to Leroy.

'Ladies and gentlemen,' he says, addressing the spectators. 'I'm afraid I've bent the rules a little, but this is for our favourite charity and I hope that you will forgive me. I was the mystery bidder. I'm afraid I couldn't resist a few hours bossing this little slut around. Any objections?'

It's a good-natured crowd and perhaps because of the charity angle no one has a problem with Leroy's blatant abuse of power. As people drift around the club to watch the new slaves and masters get acquainted, I'm left onstage with Leroy, and the knowledge that he's just paid seven grand to own my body. The closer he gets, the bigger and stronger he seems. I bow my eyes: I know the rules, I can't speak until he talks to me. I'm so keen to submit to his will that my whole body has turned to a hot liquid. I'm his. He owns me for the next four hours. What will he do to me? The thrill of knowing I have no control over what happens to me for the rest of the night is the purest exhilaration I have ever felt.

Now that it's just the two of us, Leroy's normally soft voice has a hard edge to it. He pulls me over to him by the chains that bind my wrists and ankles, and snarls into my ear. 'Okay, this is how it is,' he says. 'I own you now. So I control your pleasure. I can do whatever I want to you, but you are not allowed to take any gratification from my acts or to come until I give my permission. You may not deny any request of mine. And you may not speak unless I say so or ask a direct question. Is that clear?'

I bite my lip and nod, trying to control my breathing. The good thing about having my eyes downcast is that I can focus on Leroy's crotch. I wonder if it's as lean and mean as the rest of him. What will he do with it? Where will he fuck me? My mouth? My arse? My pussy? All three are crying out for a harsh pounding from a merci-less cock.

'Good,' he says as I nod. 'Because I've paid good money for you. I hope you won't disappoint me.'

'No, Master,' I say, and then gasp sharply as he delivers a slap to one of my tits. I watch as pink fingerprints appear on the tender pale flesh around my nipples. As the rush of his touch subsides, the other nipple begins to engorge and darken, eager to receive a similar punishment. But he is not to gratify my wishes.

'Did I give you permission to speak?' he snarls. I shake my head and he marches me over to a corner of the room where a three-walled cage stands, various hooks and chains hanging from the bars. Leroy tugs the chains that still hang from the manacles on my ankles and wrists and attaches them to four little hooks so that I'm splayed out like a starfish. My legs are as far apart as they can possibly go and it's uncomfortable from the moment I assume the position. I wonder how much more discomfort I can take. My arms are yanked half out of their sockets, causing my breasts to rise so that my nipples are tightly constricted. They now bulge out through the holes in my bra. My skirt rides up around my waist so that my pussy is out there for the world to see.

'Are you comfortable?' asks Leroy, his face deadly serious. I've been here before. Trick questions. Say no, that's what they want to hear, and they'll neglect me for the rest of the night, deny me the more extreme pleasure

I crave. Say yes, and he'll get vicious, crank it up to a level that's beyond even my depraved desires. Ah, what the fuck. I can handle it. Bring it on.

'That's very comfortable, master,' I say and as I do I wince as he pulls the chains tighter, so that I'm totally suspended now. The most intimate, vulnerable areas of my body – my inner thighs, my underarms, the underside of my breasts, oh, and my pussy – are all exposed, utterly vulnerable, his to pleasure or abuse, whichever he wants. I close my eyes and wait for the first stroke of the whip, the slap of the paddle, not knowing which instrument of torture Leroy's going to use on me first, but my whole body is alive and trembling in anticipation.

What happens instead totally unnerves me. First of all I feel warm sweet breath on my face and then a pair of soft lips is on mine. This gentle, respectful kiss shocks and thrills me more than a thousand lashes of the whip. Leroy holds still for a while and then probes my lips with his tongue, trails it across my teeth, explores the inside of my mouth while my mind races. I'm not used to this, and his soft touch is really disarming me. Then he turns his attention to my nipples: they're puffy and I yearn for his touch, his teeth on my tits, a harsh pinch, perhaps. As Leroy's head bends to my breasts I notice them stiffen and harden in anticipation of his touch. When he does take them in his mouth, his touch is as tender and sensitive as anything I've known. I feel the warmth of his lips transfer itself to my pussy, which starts to pound and throb. This slow, exquisite torture is more intense than any whip or chains. Then he's back up at my mouth, kissing me, harder this time, and it's like he's got a link directly to my clit. He takes my lower lip in his mouth and sucks gently at first, then more forcefully. As he becomes more aggressive and greedy, I'm finally receiving stimulation that I under-stand and love. This is the masterful behaviour I was expecting, that I was psyched up for. As he takes my lip between his teeth and bites down hard, I arch my back, my whole body suddenly suffused with a burning fire that only some heavy fucking will quench. For the first time, my mind forms the sentence I'll need to say but won't be allowed to cry out: 'I need to come. I need to come. I need to come.'

Leroy pulls away from me and when he does, I see a spot of blood on his lower lip. I suck my own lip and realise it's mine, he's broken the skin. A crowd are gath-ering now and I love the fact that they can all see how I've been marked by my master, branded as his property with a tiny cut on my lip and a red smear on my chin. He reaches into a bag at the foot of the cage and produces a tiny chrome rod that looks like a mascara wand. When he clicks a switch and the sleek little bar begins to buzz and hum, I know that it's not make-up he's got in mind.

Standing at arm's length – his very distance from me becomes a form of torture in itself, doesn't he know that my body is his to use and abuse? Doesn't he know how my flesh craves to be pressed up against his? – Leroy traces the vibe across my splayed body, tickling me under the arms and behind the knees. To giggle is totally forbidden, and I have to strain every nerve in my body and bite down into my own shoulder to suppress the uncontrollable squeals that build up inside me. As I buck and writhe, restrained in my bonds, I'm so wildly turned on that I can't obey my body's most basic instincts.

Then, with a firmer touch, he holds the vibe to my nipples. They tingle and throb until the extreme sensation is almost unbearable. That's when he points the silver stick between my legs, almost-but-not-quite touching my pussy lips. I'm mortified to see that a droplet of juice spills from my naked, swollen pussy and lands on the floor where it sits like a tiny pearl. For me to take pleasure from Leroy's abuse is forbidden. Will he notice? Of course he does. Nothing escapes this master's attention.

'Are you aroused?' he says, strictness in his voice. 'I don't remember giving you permission to get turned on.' I shake my head, knowing that my body has betrayed me and it's too late. He pushes the toy against my pussy lips. From my restrained position I can't see my sex, but I'm sure my pleasure must be obvious in my throbbing, pulsating pussy for all to see. Then he puts it on my clitoris. As the tension builds in my sensitive little bud, my arms and legs begin to ache and my whole body yearns for release.

'Do you want someone inside you?' asks Leroy

'Yes, Master,' I somehow find the strength to say.

'Who do you want inside you?' he demands.

'You, Master,' I half-pant, half-scream.

'How much do you want it?'

'I will die if you don't fuck me,' I say, and I mean it.

He pulls a condom from his pocket: a red rubber condom covered with ridges and nodules. I thrill at the sight of it: I'm so sopping wet that I'm going to need some rough, heavy stimulation if I'm to feel his prick inside my hole. He pushes into me roughly, mercilessly, and I feel each rubber bobble tickle and scrape the inside of my cunt. I'm so hot that it only takes two or three thrusts for it to happen: my pussy floods with clear liquid and my whole body convulses as the red-hot tremors overwhelm me.

Leroy takes me down from the manacles and I collapse into a heap in the floor, arms and legs tingling as the blood flows to them again. My body is limp and woozy with satisfaction but my mind is already reeling, so pleased with what I've just experienced that I can't help but be disappointed that it's over. Or is it? As I feel Leroy's hands grab my hair and yank me to my feet, I feel a fresh wave of excitement engulf my body.

'Come with me, slave,' he says, pulling me so hard by the hair that I have no choice but to follow where he leads me. He marches towards a private room at the back of the club, puts his hand on the door handle and turns to me with a wink and a nod to the clock. It's not quite 4 a.m. yet – not quite. 'I still own you for the next six minutes,' he says. 'And you haven't made me come yet.'